NANCY DREW MYSTERY STORIES

THE
HAUNTED BRIDGE

BY

CAROLYN KEENE

ILLUSTRATED BY

RUSSELL H. TANDY

NEW YORK
GROSSET & DUNLAP
PUBLISHERS

Made in the United States of America

P. Darfess

CONTENTS

CHAPTER		PAGE
I	An Unpleasant Companion	1
II	Sammy's Story	11
III	The Injured Hand	22
IV	Nancy's Assignment	33
V	Investigating the Ghost	42
VI	The Carved Brass Chest	51
VII	A Jeweled Vanity Case	60
VIII	The Burned Mansion	69
IX	A Mysterious Gardener	77
X	Nancy Accused	84
XI	The Crumpled Telegram	93
XII	A Clue from the Caddy	102
XIII	A Telltale Photograph	108
XIV	A Mystery Explained	113
XV	Rambling Words	117
XVI	An Unwanted Gift	124
XVII	The Missing Car	132
XVIII	Caught by the Storm	141
XIX	An Unexpected Visitor	151
XX	Gathering Evidence	160
XXI	The Note in the Fountain	170
XXII	The Chums' Help	180
XXIII	An Exoneration	189
XXIV	A Detective's Invitation	196
XXV	Farewell to the Ghost	208

"IT LOOKS LIKE A JEWEL CASE!" NANCY GASPED.
The Haunted Bridge

CHAPTER I

AN UNPLEASANT COMPANION

"OH, that was a beautiful drive, Nancy!
Your ball must have gone at least two hundred
and twenty-five yards!"

George Fayne, an attractive girl with a boy's
name, followed the flying pellet with her eyes as
she spoke, while her cousin, Bess Marvin, added
with an envious sigh:

"Yes, and straight down the fairway, too. I
wish I could drive a golf ball even half that
distance."

Nancy Drew, a pretty girl in a trim white
sports frock, smiled as she started to walk along
with her chums.

"The game of golf isn't won with a long
drive," she remarked modestly. "I've learned
never to count my score until the little ball is
safe in the cup at the end of each hole."

"You have been playing marvelously today,'

1

George insisted as she consulted the score card. "You'll certainly qualify for the tournament, if you don't let your mind wander off on the mystery your father hinted about."

The three girls were spending a few days at the Deer Mountain Hotel as guests of Nancy's father, Carson Drew, who had been called to the locality on legal business. The fashionable summer resort afforded a decided contrast to the familiar quiet of River Heights, their home town, and the girls were enjoying every minute of the vacation.

Prior to their arrival at the Deer Mountain locality, Mr. Drew had promised his daughter that she might aid him with a troublesome "case" which now was absorbing his time. As yet he had not explained the nature of the work, and during the lawyer's lengthy absences from the hotel the girls amused themselves on the golf course.

George and Bess thoroughly enjoyed the game. They both played very well, but it was Nancy's scores which had attracted the attention of the golf chairman. The man had urged her to enter the qualifying round of an important tournament to be held that week at the Deer Mountain course. Nancy had demurred, feeling that she could offer little competition to the many excellent women players who frequented the hotel, but her friends had teased her until finally she had consented to "try her luck."

"You'll most certainly qualify, Nancy!" George declared again gleefully. "This is the sixteenth hole, and only two more to go after that."

"This is a difficult one," Nancy said dubiously as she regarded the faraway green, where she would finally put her ball in the cup. "Unless I make a perfect shot, I'll go into the woods."

The girls were now walking rapidly down the fairway, and as Nancy spoke, her eyes wandered to the dense growth of forest on either side. Presently Bess and George, coming to their balls, made splendid shots. Nancy then stepped up to her own ball, and with a powerful hit with her spoon club sent it flying.

"Beautiful!" Bess cried excitedly. "Nancy, that was your longest ball of the day!"

"And one of my most disastrous, I'm afraid," the Drew girl murmured under her breath, as she saw the tiny white object sailing straight toward the tall trees.

"What miserable luck!" Bess squealed in dismay.

"Did you see the ball stop, caddy?" Nancy asked the small freckle-faced lad who was carrying her bag of clubs.

He shook his head. "I lost it just at the edge of the woods," he admitted reluctantly. "But I think it went in real deep."

"I'm afraid it did," Nancy sighed.

"We'll find your ball so you won't have to

take a penalty,'' George said confidently, as the three girls walked toward the woods.

"I hope we do," Nancy replied soberly. "I can't really afford to lose even a single stroke if I'm to qualify for the tournament."

A five minutes' search in the tall grass at the edge of the fairway did not reveal the missing ball.

"I'm certain it went deeper into the woods," Nancy Drew remarked with a troubled frown. "There seems to be a ravine back in there."

"If it ever reached the edge of the ravine it's gone forever," George admitted ruefully. "What possesses our caddies anyway? Why aren't they over here helping to look for the ball?"

The three boys had walked on toward the green.

"What good is a caddy if he doesn't help one find lost balls?" Bess added a trifle crossly.

She motioned to the boys to approach, but only Nancy's caddy reluctantly obeyed the signal.

"Don't you think you might help us look for my lost ball?" Nancy gently reproved the lad. "I'm afraid it went over toward the ravine."

"Then there's no use searching for it," the boy answered, lingering at the edge of the woods.

Nancy felt a trifle provoked. "After all, you're being paid to keep track of my ball," she said sternly.

"I'd not go into that woods if you'd give me a million dollars."

"Why?" Nancy asked, gazing at the boy in surprise. "Are you afraid of snakes?"

"Snakes and worse things."

"What could be worse than a big ugly snake?" Bess questioned with a shudder.

"Ghosts!" came the boy's unexpected reply.

"Ghosts!" Nancy exclaimed, and laughed. "Well, I'm sure there can't be any ghosts around here. What are you afraid of, anyway?"

The caddy gazed intently toward the ravine as he answered in a voice scarcely above a whisper:

"The haunted bridge. That's what I'm afraid of, and so are the other boys. You couldn't hire one of them to go near that place."

Nancy regarded the caddy incredulously. She scarcely could believe that she had heard correctly, yet she knew that the little fellow meant his words seriously for his face mirrored fear.

"A haunted bridge!" George exclaimed before either of her chums could offer a comment. "Well, now, that's something new. I've heard of haunted houses——"

"Girls, we're holding up a foursome directly behind us," Bess interrupted, glancing back over her shoulder. "Shall I signal them to drive through?"

"No, we may as well go on," Nancy decided

quickly, "or we'll be forever getting back to the hotel. I'll give up my ball as lost."

"That's the best way," the caddy declared in obvious relief. "You couldn't have played it from behind all those trees, anyway."

"It's a shame," George commented regretfully as the girls hastened on again. "You had such a splendid score up to here and now this trouble will cost you a stroke. I hate to see you have to add a point."

Nancy's thoughts were upon the remark made by her caddy. She meant to learn more from him about the haunted bridge. She would question the lad as soon as the round should be over. For a few minutes she did not keep her mind on the game, with the result that her score for the hole was six.

"Oh, you should have had a four," George murmured sympathetically.

Still thinking of the lost ball, Nancy played the next hole rather carelessly, a fact which worried her chums. As the girls walked toward the eighteenth tee they noticed that another player was there ahead of them. He was a tall, thin man in his late twenties, immaculately dressed in white slacks, with his sleek black hair plastered back from an angular, hard face.

"Oh, he's Mortimer Bartescue," Nancy said in an undertone. "Let's slow up, girls."

The warning was spoken too late. The man had seen the girls. He waved and waited for them to approach.

"Such luck!" Bess commented in disgust. "We would have to meet *him*."

Mortimer Bartescue had been presented to the girls the previous evening at the hotel, and immediately he had tried to make a golfing engagement with Nancy. Although she had heard the man was a very good player, she had found an excuse for refusing the invitation, for she had taken a dislike to him. Obviously he was a braggart, and she rather distrusted his claim that he came from an excellent family. Now, as the girls seated themselves on a bench directly behind the teeing ground, he smiled affably.

"May I have the honor of playing in with you young ladies?" he inquired engagingly, directing his smile toward Nancy.

The girls felt that they must be civil to the man, whose only real offense so far had been that he had been too friendly.

"Yes, we may as well all walk in together," Nancy replied politely but with no warmth in her voice.

She drove a straight ball, while Bess and George played somewhat shorter ones down the fairway. As the group moved along, Mortimer Bartescue attached himself to Nancy.

"You play a fine game, Miss Drew," he praised. "I've never seen a girl with such a pretty swing or for that matter——"

"Thank you," Nancy said quickly, fearing a more personal comment.

"I was just thinking that you might like to enter the mixed foursome tournament with me next week," the man went on after a slight pause. "Together we should win first place, for I'm a pretty good golfer."

"I may not be here next week," Nancy declined a trifle coldly.

"I've played golf courses all over the world," the man continued in a boasting tone. "Once I played the Prince of Wales."

"Indeed? And did you defeat him?" Nancy asked, trying to hide a smile.

"Well, yes, I did," the man admitted with a show of modesty. "But only by a couple of strokes. Oh, yes, I've often played with royalty."

By this time Nancy had reached her ball. As she was about to hit it, Mortimer moved a trifle close, and as she took her back swing, Nancy let her mind momentarily switch to him. As a result, she dubbed the shot.

"Too bad, too bad," the man muttered sympathetically. "You drew in your elbow just as you struck the ball. Here, let me show you."

He took the club from the girl's hand, and to the annoyance of the three chums insisted upon giving a demonstration of what he considered to be Nancy's fault. She said nothing, but a moment later, completely disregarding Bartescue's advice, walked to her ball and played a splendid shot.

"That's the way," Mortimer nodded.

"You'll make a five, the way the professionals do."

"I haven't made it yet," Nancy said somewhat testily, and did not speak again.

Finally her ball was only five feet from the cup. Intensely annoyed, because the man was still with her and still talking, she stepped up to putt. The shot was perfectly played, but at the very edge of the hole the ball stopped.

"Oh, Nancy! Did you ever!" Bess wailed.

Mortimer Bartescue immediately jumped up and down on the ground, causing the ball to drop into the cup.

"There, Miss Drew! Your five."

"That really wasn't fair," Nancy said severely. "I shall count that as an extra putt which gives me a six."

"But I don't see why—you didn't strike the ball——"

Nancy and her chums smiled coldly, and murmuring a few polite phrases, walked to the hotel, leaving the man to stare blankly after them.

"Of all the conceited people, he's by far the worst I've ever met!" Bess exclaimed when they were beyond Bartescue's hearing. "I'll venture to say he never came within a mile of royalty, to say nothing of defeating the Prince of Wales by two strokes!"

"And he made you miss your shot, Nancy," George added irritably. "Oh, it's a shame your score had to be ruined on the last two holes."

"You'll surely qualify, anyway," Bess said as she studied the card. "George has a hundred and two, my score is a disgraceful hundred and twenty, but Nancy has a brilliant ninety-three!"

"Did I really do that well?" the girl asked in surprise.

"It's just perfectly grand," Bess insisted. "George and I will attest to your score and then you can turn it in."

Mortimer Bartescue had followed the girls, but as they saw him coming toward them, they hastily slipped out on the veranda.

"I wonder what became of my caddy?" Nancy asked, looking about. "I meant to talk to him when I paid him."

"About the haunted bridge in the woods?" Bess inquired. "I suppose you'll want to inspect it. Well, if there's anything spooky about it, count me out on an investigation."

"I'd like to make further inquiries about the whole thing," came Nancy's reply.

"That certainly is the proper way to approach a mystery," George added. "Do you think there is anything to what the caddy said?"

"He looked genuinely frightened when he spoke of entering the woods," Nancy said musingly, "so I believe there is something to it. I'm going to locate that boy and probe into the mystery of the haunted bridge!"

CHAPTER II

SAMMY'S STORY

BEFORE the girls had an opportunity to search for Nancy's missing caddy, Mortimer Bartescue strode out upon the veranda.

"Oh, here you are," he said gaily. "I've been looking for you everywhere. I'd like you to take tea with me on the terrace."

"Thank you, but I haven't time just now," Nancy said quickly. "I must find my caddy."

"I'll go with you—" the man began, but Nancy pretended not to hear him.

She fled from the veranda, leaving Bess and George to think up their own excuses for escaping the objectionable Mr. Bartescue.

Nancy retraced her steps to the eighteenth green. Though several of the caddies were lingering near by, the little fellow who had carried her clubs was nowhere to be seen. She questioned another boy regarding him.

"Sammy Sutter caddied for you," she was told. "He's just starting out with a twosome. You might catch him at the first tee."

Nancy thanked the lad and hastened to the other part of the course, which was hidden from her view by a wing of the Deer Mountain Hotel.

11

Two men had just driven balls. As she approached them she observed Sammy starting down the fairway, heavily burdened under the weight of a huge leather bag.

"Oh, Sammy, just a minute," Nancy hailed the boy. "I want to speak with you."

The caddy obediently halted, although he glanced somewhat nervously toward the portly gentlemen whose clubs he was carrying.

"I forgot to pay you for your work this afternoon," Nancy said with a warm smile, taking some money from her pocket. "I want to ask you about that haunted bridge, too."

"I can't stop to talk now," Sammy replied, shifting his weight uneasily.

"I understand. But will you meet me near the caddy house after you have finished your work?" Nancy requested. "I'll be there about four o'clock."

"I won't be able to make it that soon. I can tell these men will be slow."

"Make it five o'clock, then. You'll not fail me, will you, Sammy?"

"No, I'll wait for you," the boy soberly promised.

He hurried off, and Nancy slowly made her way back to the hotel veranda where she found her chums still in the company of Mortimer Bartescue. The man had been entertaining Bess and George with an account of the many famous and socially prominent persons with whom he claimed to be acquainted.

"I believe I'll turn my score card in to the tournament chairman now," Nancy remarked to the girls. "If one of you will attest it——"

"Here, allow me," interrupted Mr. Bartes-cue. Before Nancy could prevent him, he had taken the score card and carefully written his name at the bottom.

The act provoked the girl, but of course she could not very well protest. As Mr. Bartescue inscribed his name, she noted a rather curious thing. It seemed to her that he formed each letter of his signature with painful precision, but she pretended not to notice this.

Nancy took the card. Then, accompanied by her chums, she offered it to the tournament chairman who was busy chartering up the results of the day's matches on a large sheet of white cardboard.

"A very fine score, Miss Drew," he praised her as he glanced at the card.

"Will she qualify for the tournament, do you think?" Bess questioned the man eagerly.

"She certainly will unless better scores come in tomorrow," he replied with a smile. "However, I don't believe the competition has ever been as keen as it is this year. Some of the best women golfers in the state are entering the tournament."

"I'll feel very fortunate if I so much as qualify," Nancy replied. "I understand there is to be a tournament for men, too."

"Yes, I have entered it," said a voice behind

the girls.   They turned to find Bartescue standing there.   "So far my score is the lowest
turned in," he added.

"That's splendid," Nancy murmured indifferently, hurrying away with her chums.

As the elevator carried the girls to their
rooms on the fourth floor, Bess and George slyly
teased Nancy about her new admirer.

"I dislike his type and you both know it," the
Drew girl replied spiritedly.   "But I must confess there was a certain something about him
which captured my interest."

"His sleek black hair?" Bess giggled wickedly.

"Don't be silly, Bess.   That fellow looks like
one of those wax models one sees in store windows.   But I was interested in the way he signed
my score card.   Did you notice how unnaturally
he wrote his signature, as if he were trying to
disguise his usual style of writing?"

"Why no," George admitted in surprise.
"You seem to observe everything, Nancy."

"I guess that's why she has solved so many
baffling mysteries," Bess sighed enviously.
"Nancy knows how to make use of her eyes and
we don't."

"I think Dad trained me to be observing,"
Nancy said modestly.

The girl was justly proud of her father,
Carson Drew, whose fame as a criminal lawyer
had spread over many states.   In a slightly different way, Nancy herself had achieved dis-

tinction, for she was a noted amateur detective with a long list of successful mystery cases to her credit.

Nancy had never intended to become a detective. Rather, the role of investigator had been thrust upon her when her father, puzzled about some details of one of his difficult cases, had permitted his daughter to assist him. Nancy had gone to work with a will, amazing everyone by her skill and cleverness in solving the Secret of the Old Clock. After that, Mr. Drew was only too glad to have her help with other baffling cases.

Nancy's adventures soon embraced many fields, but some of those which she liked best to recall had taken her to such picturesque localities as Red Gate Farm, Lilac Inn, Shadow Ranch, and Larkspur Lane. Recently she and her chums had uncovered a strange tale which centered about a queer old abandoned mansion at Sea Cliff. There the girls located a striking marble statue which many persons claimed actually resembled Nancy Drew. In solving the mystery surrounding it they were instrumental in reuniting a married couple who had been separated years before.

Nancy was an only child, but the fact that she had neither sisters nor brothers had never tended to make her selfish. She was generous to a fault, and probably was the most popular young person in River Heights. Since the death of her mother, Nancy and her father had lived alone with only Mrs. Gruen, their faithful housekeeper.

"By the way, did you learn anything about the haunted bridge?" George asked after the girls were in their rooms.

"Not yet," Nancy answered, glancing at her wrist watch, "but I have an appointment to talk with Sammy, the caddy, at five. I hope to hear the entire story then."

It was already fairly late in the afternoon, and by the time the girls had taken showers and Nancy had discarded her crumpled sports dress for a cool linen, she discovered that she would have to hurry if she hoped to reach the caddy house at the appointed hour. Sammy awaited her there, offering no comment as the girl led him to a bench at the rear of the hotel.

"Now tell me everything about the haunted bridge," she urged, trying not to appear too eager. "Why do you say that it is haunted, Sammy?"

"Because it is," the boy insisted grimly. "All of the caddies will tell you the same thing. Sometimes you can see the ghost walking over the bridge."

"At night, you mean?"

"Day time, too. It waves its arms slowly up and down."

"Have you witnessed this sight yourself, Sammy?"

"Sure. That's why I know better than to go into that woods."

"You mean you've never investigated the ghost at close range?" Nancy inquired with a smile.

"You couldn't hire any of the boys to go near the bridge. Once Pete Dalton started down there, but before he was halfway in he fell over a stone and broke his leg. After that the other fellows stayed away."

"I don't believe in ghosts myself, Sammy."

"You'd believe in this one all right if you could hear it groaning. Sometimes it screams as if it were in pain. It's enough to give a fellow the shivers. I don't even like to walk down number sixteen fairway any more."

"Tell me, is the bridge and the surrounding property owned by the hotel?" Nancy questioned.

Before Sammy could reply, the caddy master appeared and called to the boy that he was wanted immediately.

"I'll have to go now," Sammy told Nancy hurriedly.

"Thank you for telling me about the ghost," she returned. "And by the way, would you like to caddy for me in the tournament day after tomorrow?"

"Sure," the lad agreed with a broad grin. "But I won't promise to look for any balls in the woods."

After Sammy had returned to the caddy house, Nancy leisurely walked back to the hotel. As she went through the lobby a sudden thought occurred to her, and impulsively she turned to speak with the clerk at the desk.

"May I please look through the hotel register?" she requested.

"Certainly." The man pushed the book across the desk toward her.

Nancy scanned several pages until she came upon the name which she sought, that of Mortimer Bartescue. Thoughtfully she studied the man's handwriting.

"It's not a bit like the way he wrote his name on my score card," she reflected. "Obviously he disguised his signature; yet why should he wish to do so?"

Nancy was so absorbed in looking at the register that she failed to observe Mortimer Bartescue, who had come up directly behind her. Pausing, the man regarded her intently for a moment. Then, without speaking, he dodged back into a telephone booth. Without the slightest suspicion that her action had been witnessed, Nancy presently rejoined her chums upstairs.

Bess and George were dressing for dinner, but they were not too occupied to bombard Nancy with questions concerning the haunted bridge. She told them everything she had learned, but refrained from voicing her suspicions regarding Mortimer Bartescue.

Carson Drew dined with the girls that evening but Nancy noticed that he seemed more preoccupied than usual.

"Isn't your case progressing well, Dad?" she questioned him anxiously.

"Not very well so far," he replied, "but I have high hopes that things will begin to break my way soon. I'll probably need your help presently, Nancy."

"I hope so, Dad. I'm ready to go to work whenever you say."

After dinner Mr. Drew told the girls that he must absent himself from the hotel for a few hours.

"We'll manage to amuse ourselves," Nancy laughed. "There is to be a dance here this evening."

The hotel orchestra was an excellent one. The chums met many attractive young men who were vacationing at Deer Mountain. Nancy was never at a loss for a partner, and usually before a dance was finished someone cut in. Mortimer Bartescue was a persistent offender in this respect, and though he was an excellent dancer, Nancy did not care for his company.

"You are by far the most charming girl here this evening," the man said flatteringly as the music ended for one number.

He firmly steered Nancy toward the veranda. She was upon the verge of dismissing him rather curtly, when it occurred to her that she might be overlooking an opportunity to glean a few facts of interest regarding the man. He liked nothing better than to talk about himself, and by cleverly leading up to the subject of

handwriting, Nancy thought that she might induce Mortimer Bartescue to admit that he had
disguised his signature.

Accordingly, she offered no objection as the
man guided her out of the crowded ballroom to
the cool veranda. He immediately launched
into a story of his adventures in England, but
at the first opportunity Nancy switched to the
subject which was of interest to her.

In the semi-darkness she did not notice her
companion regard her shrewdly. Certainly she
had no suspicion that he was fully aware of her
purpose in bringing up the topic of handwriting.

"I've often thought that the study of graph-
ology would be interesting," Nancy said lightly.
"Some persons profess to be able to tell a
person's character by means of his handwriting."

"What an interesting tale could be built up
around mine!" Mr. Bartescue replied with a
soft chuckle. "But I fear my personality would
vary with my signature."

"Isn't one's handwriting always the same?"

"The way I write varies with my moods.
This afternoon your charm had me so baffled
I could hardly write my name at all. I doubt
that I would even recognize it on your score
card."

Nancy glanced quickly at the man but his face
was a perfect mask. She could not read what
was in his mind.

"I wish you wouldn't keep speaking of my charm, as you call it," the girl said in a nettled tone. "It really embarrasses me."

"But Miss Drew, you are so very attractive," the man insisted, moving closer. "In all my life I've never met anyone like you——"

Nancy took a step backward. She did not realize that she had been standing very close to the edge of the veranda. Suddenly her heels were no longer on solid cement and she felt herself falling.

With a startled outcry she sought to recover her balance but it was too late. Before Mortimer Bartescue could extend a hand to save her she had toppled into a flower bed.

"Miss Drew, are you hurt?" the man called anxiously, springing down from the porch to assist her.

Nancy slowly arose from the ground, trying to brush the dirt from her evening dress.

"I've sprained my hand," she admitted, fighting to keep back the tears. To herself she said, "Oh, dear, I hope this stupid fall won't mean that I'll be out of the golf tournament or that I can't help Dad on his case!"

CHAPTER III

The Injured Hand

ATTRACTED by Nancy's first cry of alarm, several persons came running from the hotel ballroom to learn what was wrong. The situation was intensely embarrassing to the girl, who could not very well explain that she had fallen from the veranda because she had been trying to avoid Mortimer Bartescue's unwelcome attentions.

Nancy was furious at the man, and it required a great deal of will power on her part to keep from speaking sharply to him. If she were unable to play in the tournament or be of help to her father, it would be entirely his fault.

"Let me see the bruise," Bartescue urged. "I don't believe it's a very bad one."

Nancy ignored him completely, and walking swiftly away, went directly to her room. The pain in her left hand was not so intense now but she could feel the fingers growing stiff.

"I'll never be able to play," she thought miserably. "Sometimes it takes weeks for a sprain to get well."

While Nancy was in the bathroom trying to

doctor her hand, Bess and George came hurrying into the room.

"Oh, Nancy," the latter wailed, "we just heard about your accident. Mortimer Bartescue said you weren't hurt, but you are!"

"Let me see the injury, Nancy," Bess cried.

"There's nothing to see. The skin isn't even broken. But I can assure you it hurts!"

"You must go straight to a doctor," George urged.

"I'm afraid it's too late. The damage is done."

"Someone should push that Bartescue man off the porch!" George said crossly. "My, how I detest that conceited prig!"

When Carson Drew returned to the hotel twenty minutes later he too became concerned over his daughter's injury, particularly when she admitted that the fall had twisted her back slightly.

"Now don't be foolish, Nancy," he said severely. "I'm going to have the house physician come up here to look at you. After all, you want to play in that golf tournament, don't you?"

"Yes," Nancy answered meekly.

Doctor Aikerman was a quiet, dignified man who had very little to say. However, the few words which he spoke after his examination were directly to the point.

"This sprain isn't serious, but you must give your hand a rest. I'll wrap it up for you and you're to leave it entirely alone for three or four days.''

''You mean I'm not to play any golf?''

''No golf.''

''But doctor—'' the girl's voice became pleading—''it really doesn't hurt very much. And the tournament starts day after tomorrow.''

''Nancy has a very good chance to win, we think,'' Bess interposed helpfully.

''Well—'' the doctor wavered as he studied Nancy with twinkling eyes—''I can see that you are a very determined young lady. I suppose you could play, although at the moment I advise against it. However, I may alter my opinion by tomorrow night.''

Doctor Aikerman picked up his black bag from the table. ''I might suggest a body massage to prevent your muscles from becoming stiff. I feel that's about the only thing that will help you.''

The idea of a massage rather appealed to Nancy, who felt battered and sore. After the physician had gone she consulted the hotel directory to see if a masseuse were available. Although one was listed, she did not answer her phone.

''Bess and I could give you a good rub,'' George volunteered.

''Did you ever give such a treatment?'' Nancy asked dubiously.

''No.'' her chum admitted frankly, ''I never

did, but there's absolutely nothing to it. You just locate the various muscles and then rub until the soreness is all gone.''

Nancy allowed herself to be persuaded. Obediently she stretched herself full length on the bed.

''Where do you hurt the most?'' George inquired sympathetically as she rolled up her sleeves ready to begin her labors.

''Everywhere,'' Nancy groaned. ''Oh, don't rub in that spot, please, George. It's too tender!''

''I have to massage the muscles,'' the Fayne girl insisted. ''Stimulating the circulation will do a lot of good and in the morning you'll feel ever so much better.''

''Where did you get that bottle of liniment?'' Nancy demanded suspiciously. ''It has a dreadful odor.''

''Say, this is a free massage so don't be so critical,'' Bess laughed. ''Put on plenty of liniment, George. It will help to take out the soreness.''

George picked up the bottle, but as she attempted to pour a little of the fluid in the palm of her hand the container slipped from her fingers, allowing at least half of the liniment to run into Nancy's hair.

''Now I'll have to have a shampoo as well as a massage,'' the girl on the bed sighed. ''I suggest we abandon the entire project.''

''I'll be more careful,'' George promised

contritely as she sopped up the liquid with a bath towel. "I don't know how that bottle slipped from my hand."

"My, that liniment must be very strong," Bess observed in awe as she gazed down at a trickle which had run on the floor. "It seems to be eating a hole in the rug!"

"And I can feel it burning a great big one in my scalp, too," Nancy insisted. "Get some water and sponge me off before all my hair is eaten away!"

Bess and George rushed frantically to the bathroom, where for several minutes they were in a panic lest their chum's lovely golden hair had been harmed. Presently, however, the effects of the liniment no longer caused any smarting, and after deciding that no real damage had been done, Nancy reluctantly allowed the massage to proceed.

Bess relieved George when the latter grew weary of her task. There was no rest or relaxation for poor Nancy. She was pummeled and pounded by her well-meaning but inexperienced chums until she felt ready to cry from sheer exhaustion.

"Oh, girls, I can't stand any more," she pleaded finally. "Just let me crawl under the covers and go to sleep."

"We're through now, anyway," Bess declared as she helped Nancy roll over on her back again. "In the morning you'll feel fine."

"I hope so," the girl groaned.

She closed her eyes, but before George could snap out the light, the telephone rang.

"It's probably Dad wanting to know how I feel," Nancy murmured drowsily.

Bess answered the call.

"It's for you, Nancy. A long distance one from River Heights."

"I wonder if anything has gone wrong at home?" Nancy said anxiously as she painfully pulled herself to a sitting position.

Bess brought the telephone to the bedside. A familiar voice at the other end of the line said cheerily:

"Hello. Nancy? This is Ned Nickerson. Can you hear me?"

"Perfectly, Ned."

"Your voice doesn't sound natural somehow," the young man complained. "I guess maybe I shouldn't have bothered you so late at night, but I thought probably you weren't having a very exciting time at Deer Mountain and would like to hear from an old friend."

"Of course I wanted to hear from you," Nancy said cordially, "but you're entirely wrong about there being no excitement at Deer Mountain."

She then told him about the haunted bridge, her unpleasant experience with Mortimer Bartescue, and finally of her misfortune in tumbling off the veranda.

"Say, I'd like to give that fellow a good punch in the jaw!" Ned replied angrily.

"You can't very well do it by long distance," Nancy laughed.

"No, but you may be seeing me sooner than you expect. In fact, that's my real reason for calling. I thought if you were planning on staying at the hotel over the week-end I might drive over with a couple of friends."

"Oh, that would be grand, Ned! And before you come will you do me a special favor?"

"Anything."

"I want you to look in the Social Register and see if Mortimer Bartescue's name is there. He claims to come from a fine family, and I'm very curious to learn if he's telling the truth."

"Say, I hope you're not getting interested in that fellow——"

"Now don't become alarmed, Ned," Nancy laughed. "Will you look up his name for me?"

"Sure thing," Ned promised, "and I'll wager it won't be there!"

A few minutes later Nancy put down the receiver, for she was very tired. George and Bess were eager to learn about the boys who were to come to Deer Mountain with Ned, but observing that their chum was too weary to talk, they turned out the lights and tiptoed away to their own room, which was adjoining.

In the morning Nancy awoke feeling greatly refreshed. Her back was not as sore as she had expected it would be though her hand still pained her.

"Will you be able to play in the tournament

do you think?'' George asked anxiously as she helped Nancy fasten her dress.

''One finger is practically useless, it's so stiff, but I certainly shall play if the doctor says I may. I'm glad I wasn't hurt so badly I couldn't help Dad.''

''Even if you do play you'll be greatly handi-capped,'' said Bess, who was always more in-terested in things which did not smack of mys-tery.

The girls had just finished dressing when a telephone call came from Mr. Drew, who wished to learn how his daughter was feeling.

''If you would enjoy it, I'd like to have you take an automobile ride with me this morning.''

''Of course I feel equal to the trip,'' Nancy answered promptly, for a certain sense of in-tuition warned her that the ride might have something to do with the mysterious ''case'' upon which her father was working. ''We'll be down to breakfast in five minutes.''

The girls were just ready to leave their rooms when a messenger boy appeared with a box of flowers for Nancy. At first she assumed that her father had sent them, but as she tore away the tissue paper from the huge bouquet of scarlet roses, a card dropped to the floor.

''Mortimer Bartescue!'' Nancy exclaimed as she read the name. She tossed the flowers care-lessly on the bed, whereupon Bess promptly rescued them.

''Even if you don't like the man, don't ruin

the flowers," she reprimanded. "I've never seen more gorgeous roses."

"They are pretty," Nancy admitted reluctantly. "I suppose he sent them because he feels responsible for me falling off the veranda."

"Wear one of the roses down to breakfast," George suggested, selecting a blossom from the vase which Bess was arranging.

"No, that would flatter the man too highly. But you girls are welcome to them."

As George and Bess pinned flowers to their dresses, Nancy went over to the table and picked up Bartescue's card once more. Turning it over, she saw that he had written a brief note of sympathy on the back.

"Girls, look at this handwriting!" she requested suddenly.

"What's wrong with it?" Bess asked, peering over her chum's shoulder.

"Does it look like the man's writing?"

"It doesn't appear to be the same signature that he attached to your score card."

"And it's not the same as the way he signed his name in the hotel register, either."

"How do you know that, Nancy?" George inquired quickly.

"Because I looked to see. I can't help feeling there's something suspicious about Mortimer Bartescue. Why should he try to disguise his handwriting?"

Nancy knew that her father was waiting for

her in the lobby, so she dropped the little card into her purse, and opened the door. The three girls hurriedly locked their rooms and went downstairs.

Directly after breakfast Nancy and Mr. Drew drove away from the hotel together, leaving Bess and George to occupy themselves with tennis and letter writing. Not until the car was some distance from the little summer resort community did the lawyer speak of the matter uppermost in his mind. He then revealed to Nancy that for the past week he had been working upon the legal angles of a smuggling case, one which had baffled New York detectives.

"For many months the authorities have been trying to break up a daring gang of jewel thieves," he explained. "It is believed that one of the members is a woman who frequents the summer resort hotels in this particular locality. Unfortunately, no description of her is available."

"Then how can you hope to trace her, Dad?"

"The assignment is a difficult one, I know, but it happens there is one good clue."

"And what is that?"

"The woman always carries an expensive jeweled vanity case, one set with diamonds and precious stones. In the back of the case is the picture of a child."

"Her own?"

"I can't answer that question, Nancy. Very little is known of this woman."

"And you say she frequents the better hotels near here?"

"Yes. For days a certain woman detective who works with me has been making the rounds, searching for her. Miss Ingle has been taken ill and will be in a hospital for at least a week. That brings me to the point I've been approaching, Nancy. How would you like to take Miss Ingle's place until she is well again?"

"I'd love it!" Nancy cried promptly.

Carson Drew nodded approvingly. He had been certain that his daughter would give an enthusiastic answer.

"When do I start work?" Nancy questioned eagerly.

"This morning," her father replied with a smile as he turned the car into a curving side road which led toward an imposing hotel overlooking a high cliff. "In just a moment now you will receive your first assignment."

CHAPTER IV

NANCY'S ASSIGNMENT

MR. DREW parked his automobile in the grounds of the Hotel Lincoln, and as he walked slowly toward the entrance with his daughter, explained what he wished her to do.

"Your work is very simple, Nancy. While I interview the hotel clerk, you are to wander about the lobby, especially the ladies' lounge, keeping an ever alert watch for a woman who might be a member of the jewel-thief gang."

"I'll look also in the powder room," Nancy promised. "A woman naturally would make use of her vanity case there."

Carson Drew nodded approvingly. They had reached the entrance of the hotel.

"We'll separate now," he advised. "I will meet you in half an hour at the car."

The lobby was fairly crowded for it was the busy season, and in this fashionable hostelry rooms were engaged months in advance. Nancy attracted no attention as she seated herself near the elevator where she might obtain a glimpse of those who entered and left.

Presently, satisfied that the woman she

sought was not on the main floor, Nancy went upstairs to loiter about in the ladies' lounge. She saw several women take vanity cases from their bags, but the little powder containers were of the plainest types.

At length the clock warned Nancy that she must return to the car to meet her father. She was there a few minutes ahead of him.

"No luck?" Mr. Drew inquired, noting the expression on her face.

"Absolutely none."

"Oh, well, we're only beginning our search," Mr. Drew responded cheerfully as he started the car engine. "An investigator's work is always tedious."

A few miles farther down the road the lawyer turned in at the grounds of Hemlock Hall, a hotel which was even larger and more exclusive than the Lincoln.

"I suppose I'm to do the same thing here?" Nancy inquired as she alighted beside her father.

"Yes, we'll meet at the car as before."

In the crowded lobby of Hemlock Hall, Nancy soon lost sight of her father. She became completely absorbed in her task of studying the various women guests, and so was a trifle dismayed when she glanced at her wrist watch some minutes later and saw that she must hurry if she were not to keep her father waiting.

"I've not even visited the powder room," she

thought. "I'll just run up there for an instant before I rejoin Dad."

The ladies' dressing room was deserted, save for the colored maid and an attractive looking woman in her early twenties. Nancy gazed at her intently and immediately was impressed by the sad expression on her face.

"She can't be the person I am after," the girl reflected. "But one can tell she's had plenty of trouble in her lifetime even if she is young."

Nancy made a pretense of arranging her hair before the mirror. Her eyes were not upon her own reflection, however, but focused themselves upon the woman who sat near by powdering her face.

Then Nancy very nearly dropped the comb in her hand, for she saw the other take from her beaded bag a beautiful vanity case which was set with sparkling gems. The Drew girl had never seen any thing like it before and instantly her heart leaped with excitement. Could it be that she had found the person for whom her father was searching?

The woman raised her eyes, flushing slightly as she became aware of Nancy's stare.

"I beg your pardon," the girl said, thinking quickly. "I don't mean to be rude, but I couldn't help admiring your vanity case. I have never seen one like it."

"Yes, it is pretty," the other agreed. "The case is one of my choicest possessions."

She casually offered it to Nancy for closer inspection. With trembling fingers the girl unfastened the catch. Would the case contain the picture of a child?

With mingled feelings of relief and disappointment, Nancy saw that the back cover was bare. It had not seemed possible to her that this dignified, quiet young woman could be a member of a disreputable gang; now she felt certain that the jeweled case had no significance. Yet there was a chance that this person, aware she was being sought, had removed the picture.

After offering a few admiring comments, Nancy returned the case, venturing to ask the woman if she were a guest at the hotel.

"No, I am not," the other admitted. "I came to take dinner with a friend. I suppose you are spending your vacation here."

Nancy was compelled to give a negative reply. She remarked that she was staying at the Deer Mountain Hotel.

"Why, I formerly lived only a short distance from that place," the woman returned in surprise. "A lovely locality. My home was destroyed by fire."

Before Nancy could inquire as to the exact location of the house or the name of the woman, the latter arose. Then, replacing the vanity case in her bag, she left the dressing room. The girl was tempted to follow her, but decided against this since she could think of no pretext for reopening the conversation. Instead, she went to the car and found her father waiting for her.

"You're late, Nancy," he chided. "I'm afraid we'll not have time to visit another hotel, for I must get back to Deer Mountain for an important interview."

"I'm sorry I kept you waiting, Dad. I'd not have done it, only I thought I had located the woman we were looking for."

She then gave a detailed description of the jeweled case which had attracted her attention. Mr. Drew, after hearing an account of the entire conversation, was inclined to agree with her that the woman probably had no connection with the smuggling case, but he did not blame his daughter for prolonging her hotel stay.

"Every clue is worth investigating," he assured her, "and it's barely possible this woman may not be as innocent as she pretends. You didn't inquire her name?"

"I had no opportunity. She told me she formerly lived near our hotel but that her home had burned."

"I'll make further inquiry when we return," Mr. Drew declared. He glanced at his watch. "We must be starting back too or I'll be late for my appointment."

"I'm afraid I wasn't much help today, Dad."

"Quite the contrary, Nancy," her father praised. "You did splendidly. I didn't expect to solve the case in one morning, you know."

At the Deer Mountain Hotel they parted company, and Nancy sought her chums who were resting in their room after several hours of vigorous exercise on the tennis courts.

"You were gone such a long while we very nearly gave you up for lost, Nancy," George declared as the girl threw herself down into a comfortable chair. "Tired?"

"Oh, a little, and my hand is hurting me again."

"You haven't been to the doctor yet?" Bess questioned anxiously.

"No, I'll probably see him this evening—I'm almost afraid of his verdict."

"If you can't play in the tournament it will be downright mean," Bess said feelingly. "Scores have been coming in all day, but the last we heard you were still in the upper group."

"There seems to be considerable gossip going the rounds about Mortimer Bartescue," George contributed. "He's playing in the men's tournament, and his qualifying score was one of the lowest turned in. Another player, the former state champion, practically accused him of cheating."

"I wish I had refused to allow the man to attest my score," Nancy said with a frown. "His word seems to mean nothing."

"Since you went away he has telephoned twice," Bess remarked teasingly. "We told him you'd probably be back about two o'clock."

"It's after that now so he'll very likely be calling again and I don't want to talk with him," Nancy sighed. "Let's go for a little walk."

"It would be just our luck to encounter him," George replied. "Where could we go?"

"I had in mind exploring the woods near the sixteenth fairway," Nancy answered quietly. "I'll not be satisfied until I've visited Sammy's haunted bridge."

"Let's get started right away!" George cried enthusiastically, looking about for her hat.

"I think we shouldn't go there alone," Bess murmured nervously. "If the caddies are afraid——"

"Now don't be a silly little goose," George said to her cousin. "You know very well there are no ghosts. It's only a story, of course."

"Stories seldom originate out of nothing," Bess retorted feelingly. "I'm just certain we'll get into trouble, but I suppose I'll have to go!"

Nancy and George merely laughed at her fears. By the time the girls reached the edge of the woods Bess began to share their zest for the adventure.

"As I recall, this was the place where my ball entered the woods," Nancy pointed out after taking careful bearings. "It bounced to the right of that big oak tree."

She led the way into the gloomy woods, closely followed by her chums.

"I'd suspect that the bridge would be down by the ravine somewhere," George commented uneasily.

"I can see something white through the trees," Nancy replied, halting. "Yes, I believe it must be the bridge."

"Maybe it's the ghost," Bess muttered under her breath.

Nancy and George courageously pushed on through the dense tangle of underbrush, with Bess bringing up the rear.

"Let's go back to the hotel," she pleaded, but her friends did not hear her.

By this time the three girls were close enough to see the bridge which was half screened by overhanging bushes. It was a sagging, old-fashioned structure, once white but now in need of both paint and repairs.

Suddenly Nancy, who was in the lead, abruptly halted, her attention held by something which lay just ahead. Bess gave a gasp of horror.

"The bridge *is* haunted!" she cried. "You can see the ghost moving slowly across it."

"The thing is waving its arms back and forth just as Sammy claimed," George added, her courage rapidly ebbing away. "Nancy, this is no place for us. Let's get out of here."

"Nonsense, George! I'm surprised at you. We came to investigate the haunted bridge, not to run away at the first suggestion of anything supernatural. Besides, I don't believe that white object can be anything so very dreadful.''

"What do you think it is?" Bess asked in a calmer tone.

"Certainly not a ghost. It might be a piece of white cloth fluttering in the breeze."

"It *might* be," Bess admitted in a frightened whisper, "but did you ever hear a piece of cloth moan and groan? Just listen!"

"I don't hear anything—" Nancy began, and then the words died in her throat.

From far down in the ravine, seemingly near the old haunted bridge, there issued a fearful cry which was like no human sound. Tortured and weird, it rose to a labored crescendo and then, as if heavy with remorse for some dreadful sin, it faded away in a lingering wail into the dim recesses of the black forest.

CHAPTER V

INVESTIGATING THE GHOST

FOR several minutes the three girls huddled together, listening for the weird sound to be repeated. Through the screen of trees they could still see the white, ghost-like object moving its arms slowly to and fro.

"Let's go back to the hotel," Bess urged nervously. "I've lost all interest in the haunted bridge."

"Well, I haven't," Nancy rejoined quickly. "Come on, girls, we'll approach very quietly and see if we can surprise the ghost."

Bess pleaded with her chums to give up the adventure, but they paid not the slightest attention to her. Rather than be left behind, she reluctantly trailed them deeper into the woods.

Nancy, who was in advance of the others, moved stealthily forward, taking care not to step on brittle sticks nor to make any sound which would betray her presence. Suddenly she halted, and to the astonishment of Bess and George, began to chuckle.

"Girls, Sammy's so-called ghost is nothing but an old scarecrow!"

"A scarecrow!" Bess echoed incredulously.

"See for yourself." Moving slightly aside, Nancy pointed toward the bridge directly below. Her chums were now close enough to it to observe a tattered white figure flapping back and forth in the breeze.

"Well, did you ever!" George exclaimed. "I guess that was a good joke on us."

No longer afraid, the girls hastened down into the ravine to examine the scarecrow. It had been set up at the entrance to the narrow, sagging bridge, though for what purpose they were unable to guess. Evidently the figure had been standing out in the open many months, for the white clothing was grimy and torn, and straw stuffing protruded from the shirt bosom. The scarecrow was so wobbly that the slightest breeze or any vibration of the bridge caused it to move. From a distance it was not surprising that the swaying motion of the arms seemed life-like.

"Well, I guess the mystery of the haunted bridge is solved," Bess said in relief.

"How do you explain the groaning sound we heard?" George asked. "I'm certain we didn't imagine it."

"No," Nancy answered gravely as she tested the bridge to see if it would bear her weight, "those moans were very real. And we know they didn't come from this scarecrow, either!"

"How do you account for it, Nancy?" Bess questioned nervously. "You don't suppose we heard the creaking of the bridge as it swayed in the wind?''

Nancy shook her head. "Those sounds couldn't have been made that way, I'm sure.''

"It's barely possible some prankster may be at work around here,'' George suggested, gazing thoughtfully about her.

Nancy held the same opinion. After the girls had searched the vicinity carefully they were more bewildered than before since there was no evidence the bridge had been visited lately.

"There's not a soul here now,'' Nancy observed, "but of course we know some person must have set up the scarecrow. For what purpose, I wonder?''

"There are no fruit trees near by and no crops to protect,'' Bess commented. "It seems fairly obvious that someone wanted to keep folks from crossing the bridge.''

"Either that, or else the scarecrow was set up for a joke,'' Nancy said slowly. "But still we can't explain those moaning sounds. Shall we cross over to the other side of the ravine?''

"The bridge doesn't look safe to me,'' Bess protested. "When you stepped on it a moment ago it sagged dreadfully.''

"I think it will hold me,'' Nancy returned, but Bess and George would not permit her to make the test.

"There's nothing to see on the other side, anyway,'' Bess declared indifferently. "Let's look for your golf ball, Nancy.''

"That probably would be a more profitable occupation. I'd like to find that ball, for it was one of my best ones. Jimmy Harlow, the champion, autographed it for me."

"Then by all means let's search for it," George responded quickly. "It should be here somewhere not far from the bridge."

The girls poked about among the bushes for nearly fifteen minutes. Though they found two water-soaked balls, they could not locate the one Nancy had lost.

"Maybe it rolled into the creek bed," Bess presently suggested.

Nancy, who wore an old pair of shoes with spikes, scrambled down the muddy bank to search.

"It's terribly slippery, girls, so don't try to follow me," she warned. "I doubt that the ball can be found here anyway, for it must be buried in mud."

A brief search convinced Nancy that she was only ruining her shoes and stockings. Deciding to rejoin her companions who were watching from above, she walked along the creek's edge looking for a place where the bank was not so steep. Suddenly her eye fell upon a metal object which was half buried in the thick mud.

"Is that your ball?" George called eagerly.

"No, it's a piece of brass—I think I've found an old plate!"

"A brass plate!" Bess exclaimed in wonder.

Meanwhile Nancy had pried up the object, and saw that it was not a plate at all but a tiny carved chest. The discovery was such an exciting one that for a moment she could only stare at the curious little brass container.

"It looks like a jewel case!" she gasped, holding up the article so that Bess and George might see it. "And it's very heavy."

"How did a thing like that get buried in the mud?" George asked blankly. "Nancy, you certainly were born lucky. You lose a golf ball and find a treasure chest!"

"It feels heavy enough to contain gold," Nancy declared in satisfaction, turning the curious object over in her hands. She estimated that the little chest was not more than six inches in length. It appeared to be approximately four inches wide and slightly less in depth.

Bess and George slipped down the muddy bank to join their chum. They were even more thrilled than she was over the strange discovery.

"Open it quickly," Bess urged. "You may have found something valuable."

"The chest seems to be locked."

"Jerk the lid, Nancy," George advised. "Maybe it's only stuck."

Nancy attempted a second time to do so but she could not open the mysterious little box.

"Let me try," George requested. She had no better success.

"It's locked, all right," Bess declared gloomily. "Maybe we can smash the lid with a rock."

"Brass won't be easy to smash," Nancy replied. "Besides, I don't want to ruin such an attractive little chest. It will be beautiful when it is cleaned and polished."

"But it's irritating not to know what it contains," George complained. "What would you say is hidden inside, Nancy?"

"I have no idea, of course, but it might be something valuable. The thing that interests me is, why was it secreted here by the haunted bridge, and by whom?"

"Perhaps the creek washed it down from higher land," Bess suggested meditatively. "The water evidently has been much higher than it is now."

"That's very possible," Nancy admitted. "Still, it seems more reasonable to me that someone deliberately buried the chest—perhaps the same person who set up the scarecrow."

"Why do you think that?" asked George.

"Oh, it's only a vague theory. Certainly I have no evidence to support my belief."

"Well, it's too deep a mystery for me," Bess declared as the girls climbed out of the ravine with their "treasure." "If Nancy can find the answer to this riddle she will be good!"

"I mean to try at least," her chum replied with a gay laugh. "Just now my main ambition is to get this little chest to the hotel without being seen by anyone. Let's enter by the rear door.''

The three soon emerged from the woods. They met no one as they cut across the golf course, but as they approached Deer Mountain Hotel they were observed by Mortimer Bartescue, who was sipping a cool drink under an umbrella table. He quickly arose and came toward the girls.

''Oh, that pest will be certain to see the chest and ask a million prying questions!'' Nancy murmured apprehensively. ''And it's too late to avoid him.''

Bess was carrying an extra sweater. Thinking quickly, she carelessly tossed it over Nancy's arm so that the brass chest was concealed completely.

''Oh, hello,'' Bartescue greeted the girls as he came up to them, ''have you been out on the golf course?''

''We were looking ffor one of my favorite balls,'' Nancy returned politely. ''I lost it in the woods the last time I played.''

''It's really too hot for golf today anyway,'' the man said, falling into step. ''May I carry your sweater, Miss Drew?''

''Oh, no,'' Nancy answered in confusion, ''I'd rather have it swinging along on my arm.'' As she observed that he was gazing at her somewhat curiously, she added hastily, ''I believe I haven't thanked you for the beautiful flowers you sent to me. It was very thoughtful of you.''

"You liked the roses?" Bartescue beamed. "I ordered the best I could get, but of course the florist shops here at Deer Mountain are not on a par with those of New York or the Continent. How are you feeling today, Miss Drew?"

"Very well, except for my hand. One finger is still quite useless.''

"You plan to play in the tournament regardless?"

"Yes, if the doctor says I may, and providing that I qualify.''

"Oh, haven't you heard?" Bartescue inquired with a smile. "Your score was one of the lowest turned in. You qualified easily for the first flight.''

"I hoped I might, but I couldn't be certain until all of the scores were in. I assume you plan to compete in the men's tournament tomorrow?"

"Oh, yes, and I'm counting upon winning the cup!" Mr. Bartescue announced confidently. "I went out for a practice round this morning and shot a nice sixty-nine.''

"Sixty-nine!" Bess echoed in amazement.

"I'm just coming into my game,'' the man boasted. "I doubt if anyone will prove a match for me unless I take an unexpected slump.''

The girls found such outrageous bragging

decidedly distasteful. Though they listened
with a show of polite interest, they did not believe that Mr. Bartescue had ever made as low
a score as he claimed. Nancy was still nervous
lest the man see the carved brass chest which
she was hiding beneath the sweater.

"Won't you take tea with me?" he invited
as the four reached the hotel entrance. He
looked a trifle offended when Nancy declined.

"Well, at least he didn't see the brass
chest," Bess chuckled as the girls gained the
privacy of their bedrooms. "I'm nearly eaten
up with curiosity to learn what is hidden inside."

Nancy tried to pry open the metal box with
a nail file but the lid would not budge. Other
tools at hand were equally worthless.

"We need something with a sharp point,"
George declared as she studied the little chest
in deep perplexity. "If only we had an ice
pick or a nail——"

Nancy sprang to her feet, her eyes alight
with excitement.

"I know what we can use, girls! Why didn't
I think of it before?"

Without waiting to explain, she dropped the
little chest into George's lap and ran from the
room.

CHAPTER VI

THE CARVED BRASS CHEST

As Nancy hurried through the hotel lobby, bent upon finding an object with which to pry open the lid of the carved brass chest, she chanced to pass a flower shop, and felt she must stop a moment to admire the beautiful display of blooms in the window.

"It would be nice to send Bess and George each a bouquet," she mused. "They admired my roses so much and they have no flowers of their own."

Impulsively she entered the shop, where she purchased two corsages of fragrant violets to be delivered immediately to her friends.

"Shall I include your name?" the clerk inquired politely as he wrapped up the flowers.

"No, just write 'From a Friend'," Nancy replied, thinking that it would be fun to tease her chums.

She did not wish to make out the cards herself, knowing that Bess and George immediately would recognize her handwriting. She watched as the clerk put down the dictated words. Nancy picked up one of the cards and looked at it curiously.

"Is that the way you wish it?" the man inquired politely.

"Yes, you have done it exactly right. It was your handwriting which interested me. Haven't I seen it before?"

"I sometimes pen cards for my customers. Perhaps someone sent you flowers from my shop."

"I did receive a bouquet of roses only yesterday from a man named Mortimer Bartescue."

"Oh, yes, I remember him. Are you Miss Nancy Drew?"

"Yes, I am."

"I wrote the card that went with your flowers," the clerk recalled. "Mr. Bartescue especially requested me to do it."

"I see," the girl murmured, without disclosing by her tone that the information had any special significance. "I was certain I had seen this handwriting before, but now I understand why it looks familiar."

She paid for the corsages and left the flower shop, hurrying directly to the caddy house where her golf bag and spiked shoes were. Bess and George were decidedly mystified when their chum returned to the hotel triumphantly bearing the latter.

"What do you intend to do with those shoes?" Bess asked curiously. "We thought you went after some sort of tool that would help to open up the brass chest."

"Could you ask for a better implement than a sharp spike?" Nancy laughed. "Just watch me. I'll soon have that chest unfastened."

Holding the metal container firmly between her knees, she held one shoe so that she could insert a row of the spikes on the bottom of it under the edge of the lid. She used the other shoe as a hammer.

"Now that's an idea!" Bess cried in delight. "I do believe it will work, too."

Nancy likewise was hopeful. However, the little chest suddenly slipped from between her knees and crashed heavily to the floor.

"Gracious!" George exclaimed. "It must contain lead to thud like that."

"I only hope the person who has the room beneath us doesn't register a complaint at the office," Nancy chuckled. "This spiked shoe is an excellent implement, but the lid seems to be downright stubborn."

"It's almost dinner time, too," Bess declared, glancing at the clock. "Shouldn't we start dressing?"

"We might have food sent up here," Nancy suggested, for she was absorbed with the riddle of the unopened chest and disliked to give up her work even for an hour.

"Bess and I thought we'd wear our new dinner frocks," George said somewhat apologetically. "Of course, if you'd rather not go downstairs——"

"No, this chest can wait," Nancy decided

instantly. She added mischievously, "You're not by any chance dressing up to impress new swains?"

"Certainly not," Bess returned haughtily.

The girls had just finished dressing when a boy appeared at the door bearing two square boxes from the florist shop.

"They're for Nancy, of course," Bess sighed wistfully. "Mortimer Bartescue is a pest but at least he's generous with his money."

"Why, these boxes are addressed to us, Bess," George cried in surprise as she took the parcels from the boy at the door. "There must be some mistake."

Nancy thoroughly enjoyed herself as she watched the girls open the boxes. So far they had no suspicion that she had sent the flowers.

"Oh, such a lovely corsage!" Bess exclaimed in delight, burying her face in the violets. "It will be just right to wear with my new dress. But who could have sent it?"

George was peering at the attached card.

" 'From a friend'," she read in a mystified tone.

"And mine is just the same," Bess said in bewilderment. "We don't know anyone who would send us flowers."

"Are you sure you haven't been hiding something from me?" Nancy inquired teasingly.

Bess and George earnestly assured her that they had no admirers at the Deer Mountain

Hotel. Nancy's broad smile betrayed her part in the affair.

"You sent these flowers, Nancy Drew!" Bess suddenly accused. " 'Fess up!"

"Well, yes, I did. I must admit I am the mysterious friend."

"The corsages will give a finishing touch to our new dresses," George declared. "It was nice of you to do this, Nancy."

"I did myself a good turn too by visiting the florist. I found out some interesting information about Mortimer Bartescue."

Nancy then explained how she had learned that the man had not written the note which accompanied the roses.

"He seems to be afraid someone will recognize his handwriting," Bess remarked thoughtfully. "Do you suppose he could be a fugitive from justice?"

"He seems to have plenty of money and no visible means of support," Nancy acknowledged. "Still, it has never occurred to me that he is the criminal type. I've thought of him merely as an annoying boaster."

Soon the girls were ready to go down to dinner.

"Why don't you wear some of Mr. Bartescue's flowers, Nancy?" Bess suggested, taking a spray of roses from the vase. "They would set off your dress beautifully."

"I don't want to flatter the man by doing that. If I should wear the roses he'd assume at once that I look with favor upon his attentions.''

"Oh, probably he'll not even be in the dining room,'' George answered carelessly. "Flowers are flowers, Nancy. Here, let me pin them on you.''

Her chum offered another protest, but finally permitted George to have her way. Since Mr. Drew had not returned to the hotel the girls planned to dine alone. They were escorted by the head waiter to a pleasant table near the window.

"Oh, there is Mr. Bartescue,'' Nancy murmured to Bess as she noticed the man sitting alone at a table near by. "I was afraid he'd be here. Don't let on you see him, girls.''

It was impossible to ignore the man for he immediately got up and came over to their table. He noticed at once that Nancy was wearing his roses, and the glance he bestowed on her was more than a friendly one.

"May I join you?'' he asked. Then, without waiting for an affirmative reply, he seated himself in the empty chair beside Nancy.

The dinner was not a pleasant affair for the girls, but Mortimer Bartescue enjoyed himself thoroughly. He idled over his food as he recounted fantastic adventures which he had experienced in Africa. From the glib way the man talked Nancy felt certain that he had never once visited that country.

At length, however, the meal came to an end.

With feelings of relief the girls left the dining room.

"Of course you're staying downstairs for the dancing, Miss Drew?" Bartescue asked Nancy as he hovered at her elbow.

"No, I must visit the doctor," she answered shortly. "He is to examine my hand again and give his verdict as to whether or not I can play in the tournament."

"You are very courageous, Miss Drew. Few girls would wish to enter competition with such a handicap."

Nancy offered no response. With a polite smile of farewell she moved away with her chums.

As Doctor Aikerman examined the injured hand, the three girls waited in anxious silence. He asked Nancy a question or two regarding the pain, and she assured him a trifle too eagerly that the injured fingers scarcely hurt at all.

"I can see you want to play," the doctor smiled.

"Please, don't you think you might grant me permission?" Nancy asked pleadingly. "Only one finger is stiff now and I'll be as careful of it as I can."

Doctor Aikerman did not immediately reply as he busied himself re-bandaging the hand. Nancy's face fell for she felt certain he did not intend to give his consent. She was greatly relieved when he said abruptly:

"I'll permit you to do it upon one condition."

"And what is that?"

"You must not remove this bandage."

Nancy frowned slightly as it occurred to her that she scarcely could hope to make her best score if her hand were encumbered with protective wrappings.

"I agree to the condition," she replied reluctantly.

"And another thing," the doctor added severely. "If your hand begins paining you after you have started to play, you must default your match. Otherwise I'll not be responsible for your case."

Nancy and her chums were rather subdued as they went to their rooms.

"I think perhaps you shouldn't try to enter the competition," Bess ventured sympathetically. "If you are unable to make a good score, folks won't realize that it is because of an injured hand. It's no disgrace to default."

"I want to play in the tournament," Nancy replied grimly. "My heart is set upon it."

"Then if you're determined to do it, the best thing is to go to bed and get all the rest you can," George advised kindly. "You'll need every bit of your strength."

"I have work to do before I go to bed," Nancy laughed. With a nod of her head she indicated the carved brass chest.

"Let Bess and me try to open it," George

urged. "Here, give me that spiked shoe, Nancy. You're apt to hurt your hand again."

Unwillingly Nancy gave up the shoe, watching eagerly as her friends took turns prying at the stubborn lid of the mysterious box. Several times they were tempted to abandon the work in disgust, but when they saw that their chum meant to take it over, quickly changed their minds.

"I believe the lid is loosening!" Bess suddenly cried. "Yes, it's coming!"

With great restraint, for she was very desirous of looking inside the container, she placed the chest on Nancy's lap.

"You shall have the honor of opening it," she said generously. "You were the one who found it."

"It's probably filled with worthless trash," Nancy laughed, but her hand trembled as she slowly raised the loosened lid.

The girls stared down into the interior, their eyes fastening in awe upon the amazing contents. For several moments there was an unbroken silence. Nancy was the first to recover from astonishment.

"It's almost unbelievable!" she murmured in a half whisper. "I never dreamed that the chest would contain anything like this!"

CHAPTER VII

A Jeweled Vanity Case

THE carved brass box was filled to the very top with jewelry. Even a casual glance assured Nancy and her chums that it was not imitation. There were necklaces of red and green and blue stones, rings with curious settings, and many other pieces rich in gold and silver.

"Why, all this must be worth a fortune," Bess murmured in awe. "Nancy, you'll be wealthy!"

"The jewelry isn't mine just because I chanced to find it."

"The owner may never be located," George said hopefully as she lifted a silver bracelet from the chest and held it up for the others to admire. "Did you ever see a more stunning thing?"

"How about this diamond ring?" Bess asked, seizing gleefully upon a little gold band set with a beautifully cut stone.

Nancy was attracted by a green necklace, but as she carefully lifted it from the chest she saw an object lying beneath it which was of far greater interest to her. The article was a jeweled vanity case!

Bess and George were so busy admiring the pieces in their hands that they scarcely noticed their chum as she caught up the tiny powder container and eagerly opened it. As she gave a sharp exclamation their attention shifted back to her.

"Girls, just see what I've found!"

Nancy held open the vanity case so that her friends might gaze at a curious picture fitted into the back cover.

"It's a photo of a child," Bess declared.

"Evidently ruined by water," George observed. "It looks like a picture of a little girl to me."

She and Bess could not imagine why Nancy should consider the discovery so important, for they felt that the photograph was worthless as a means of identifying the former owner of the vanity case. Their chum was tempted to tell them of the search her father was conducting to locate the possessor of just such an article, but recalling that the secret was not hers to reveal, she remained silent.

"You don't seem very excited over all this treasure," Bess complained as she and George continued to examine the beautiful pieces.

"I was just thinking——" Nancy answered absently.

Preoccupied, she turned the case over and over in her hand. All means of tracing the woman whom the detectives sought now had been lost. That fact was self-evident to the girl's clear, quick mind—provided the jeweled trinket was actually the woman's property. While Nancy had no concrete proof, she was fully satisfied in her own mind as to its ownership.

"I must show Dad the case just as soon as he returns to the hotel," she thought. "This chance discovery may alter all his plans."

Bess and George brought up the question of what should be done with the treasure. They were afraid to sleep with the jewelry in their room, fearing that someone might steal it during the night.

"I'll give the chest to Dad for safekeeping," Nancy declared. "He'll probably have it locked up in the hotel vault."

Shortly after eleven o'clock the girls heard Mr. Drew enter his room directly across the hall. Nancy lost no time in going to him with the carved brass chest. She threw open the lid, enjoying his look of amazement as he beheld the dazzling display of gems.

"My word, Nancy, have you been robbing a jewelry store?"

The girl laughed and explained briefly how the chest had come into her possession. She climaxed her startling tale by thrusting the jeweled vanity case into his hand.

"Dad, do you suppose this can be the article we've been trying to trace?"

Carson Drew carefully examined the gleaming object. He weighed his words carefully as he spoke in an attempt to seem calm, yet Nancy could tell that he too was excited over the discovery.

"It certainly fits the description as given to me by New York detectives. And there's no question about the quality of the jewelry."

"The chest may have been hidden by a member of the jewel-theft gang, Dad."

"Yes, that's very possible. This discovery may change all our plans."

"The mysterious woman will become more elusive than ever."

"If this vanity case belongs to her—yes. We have no other reliable clue."

"What will you do with the jewelry, Dad?"

"Keep it in my possession until I've had time to communicate with New York detectives. I'll send off a telegram immediately giving a description of every piece found in the chest. Possibly it can be identified as stolen jewelry."

"I'll be glad to turn the cache over to you," Nancy said with a smile. "I don't care for the responsibility of keeping it myself."

She kissed her father goodnight, and after telling him that she planned to play in the first round of the golf tournament the following day, hastened off to bed. Nine o'clock the next morning found Nancy waiting at the first tee for Miss Gray, the young woman whose name had been drawn with her own for the initial match.

Bess and George were on hand to see their chum drive off, but they had decided against following her over the course, fearing that their presence might prove disturbing. Nancy had arranged for Sammy to carry her clubs, and the little fellow smiled encouragingly as she took a few practice swings.

"How does your hand feel?" George inquired anxiously.

"Oh, fine," Nancy answered carelessly, for she intended to offer no excuses for herself.

Miss Gray soon arrived with her caddy and drove off a ball which sped two hundred yards straight down the fairway. If Nancy were dismayed she did not show it. She stepped calmly to the tee and sent her own ball within a few feet of that of her opponent.

Bess and George were delighted at the beautiful shot. From the first tee they watched the pair play the hole and were almost certain that Nancy had won by a stroke.

"She's starting off pretty well even if her hand does bother her," Bess declared gleefully. "Oh, I hope she takes the match."

Miss Gray was an able player and did not waste strokes. She took the second hole and the third, leaving Nancy upon the defensive. After that it was a grim fight with first one player having the advantage and then the other. Ultimately, superior skill began to

triumph, and when Miss Gray shot a ball into
the river on the fifteenth fairway the Drew
girl knew that she herself would win the match.

"You have played a beautiful game," Miss
Gray congratulated her. "You deserve to
win."

"I'm afraid my score won't be very good,"
Nancy returned. "That is, not unless I make
pars on the last three holes. Number sixteen
isn't my favorite, either."

She smiled significantly at Sammy, who
averted his eyes in embarrassment. He was
still ashamed because he had refused to search
for her lost ball.

Nancy sent a long ball flying down the fairway, and was very glad to see that it would
not enter the woods. As she walked along with
her caddy beside her, the girl could not resist
telling him that she and her chums had investigated the haunted bridge.

"And nothing happened to you?" he demanded fearfully.

"Your so-called bridge has no ghost,
Sammy."

"But I've seen the—the thing moving
about."

"What you saw through the trees was a
white scarecrow. Someone had set it up at
the entrance to the bridge."

"A scarecrow?" the lad demanded with a
short laugh. "Well, that's a good joke on all
the fellows. We were sure it was a ghost be-

cause we could hear the thing groaning. But how do you explain that? A scarecrow can't groan, can it?''

Nancy answered Sammy's question by suggesting that he may have heard the moaning of the wind. This explanation seemed to satisfy the boy.

''Say, I'm sorry I wouldn't look for your lost ball the other day,'' he apologized. ''If I were sure you were right about the ghost I'd do it yet.''

''I think you ought to,'' Nancy said, smiling in amusement because she saw that Sammy was torn by conflicting emotions. He wished to locate the golf ball, yet he could not rid himself of fear. ''I'd like especially to recover it because the ball was autographed by Jimmy Harlow,'' she added.

''Gee, I don't wonder you want to get it back,'' Sammy murmured enviously. ''Not many folks can boast of a ball with the name of that star on it. I'll look for it, Miss Drew, honest I will.''

''Have you always lived near the Deer Mountain Hotel?'' Nancy questioned the lad somewhat curiously as they were playing the last hole.

''Sure,'' the boy grinned, ''all my life.''

''Then you must know nearly everyone for miles around. Tell me, did you ever hear of a house close by the hotel which burned recently?''

The caddy looked slightly puzzled a moment, then light broke over his face.

"Oh, you must mean the Judson mansion. At one time it stood over there."

With a sweep of his brown arm, Sammy pointed back toward the woods.

"I don't suppose the house was anywhere near the bridge?"

"It was fairly close. On the other side of the ravine. It burned more than two years ago in the middle of the night. No one knew how the fire started."

"You say a Judson family lived in the house?"

"Not a family. Only Miss Margaret."

"And is Miss Margaret an old lady?" Nancy inquired with interest.

"Oh, no, she was one of the prettiest girls around. She'd be about twenty-three or four now."

"Is she dead, Sammy?"

"Not that I ever heard. Her folks died, and she was engaged to marry some fellow—a professor at a college near here. But they were never married. After the fire Miss Margaret ran away and no one heard much about her after that."

"It was odd that she disappeared directly after the fire," Nancy remarked thoughtfully.

"Yes, but the Judsons were queer folks. Some said she was stuck-up, but I guess that was because they couldn't find out anything about the family. My mother could tell **you** a lot.''

''And where does your mother live?'' Nancy asked quickly, determined to trace down every clue.

Sammy gave her the address which she wrote on the back of her score card.

''I'll certainly call at your home within a day or two to talk to your mother,'' she said.

Nancy felt highly elated over the information, for it was the first tangible clue she had secured regarding the identity of the woman with whom she had talked at Hemlock Hall. She only hoped that Sammy's mother would be able to tell her more regarding Miss Margaret, facts perhaps which would connect her with the jewel cache discovered so near the Judson home.

CHAPTER VIII

The Burned Mansion

Bess and George were waiting at the eighteenth green when Nancy and her opponent ended their play. They fell upon their chum the instant that Miss Gray was out of hearing, congratulating her upon winning the match.

"We knew you'd do it, Nancy," Bess declared proudly. "Tomorrow you'll win the second round, and then you'll be well on your way toward the championship!"

"It will not be that easy, I fear," Nancy replied soberly. "The second match is always harder than the first, although Miss Gray was a very able opponent."

"How was your score?" George inquired, taking the card from Nancy's hand.

"Not very good. I came in just a few strokes under a hundred. I figure I must get down into the eighties at least to win the tournament."

"Oh, you can do it, Nancy," Bess said confidently. "Did your hand pain you very much?"

"I was conscious of it most of the time,"

Nancy admitted ruefully, "but I'm hoping my finger won't be so stiff tomorrow."

"How about having luncheon, girls?" George suggested as the three walked arm in arm from the green.

"An excellent idea," Nancy approved. "Perhaps if we have it early we'll avoid meeting Mortimer Bartescue."

The three friends were relieved to find the hotel dining room practically deserted. After enjoying a leisurely meal they once more wandered out of doors. Nancy's gaze roved thoughtfully toward the sixteenth fairway.

"You're not considering more golf?" George asked in surprise.

Nancy shook her head. "No, eighteen holes is enough for me today. I was just thinking——"

"About the haunted bridge, I'll venture," Bess interrupted with a chuckle. "Isn't one visit to that place enough?"

"Sammy was telling me about an old mansion which burned a couple of years ago," Nancy explained, speaking as if she had not heard her chum's remark. "The place is over there in the general direction of the bridge."

"We've seen ruined houses before," George said. "Wouldn't it just be a long walk in the hot sun?"

"Not for me," Nancy rejoined mysteriously. "I'd like very much to see the spot."

She would have set off alone, but George

and Bess insisted upon accompanying her even
though the excursion was not entirely to their
liking. The three were just cutting across
number eighteen fairway when they encountered Mortimer Bartescue.

"Hello," he called cheerily, "where away
now?"

"Oh, just off for a little hike," Nancy replied lightly.

Mortimer Bartescue fell into step with the
girls.

"I have a little time to kill before I play my
match this afternoon. I may as well walk
along."

The chums glanced at one another in con-
sternation. If Bartescue should insist upon
accompanying them they must quickly alter
their plans.

"I doubt if we'll be back very soon," Nancy
said pointedly. "You might miss your
match."

"Oh, I can always turn back if I see it is
getting late. Where are we going, anyway?"

"Just walking," Nancy answered crossly.
"And if you don't mind, Mr. Bartescue, we'd
prefer to keep this a threesome."

"In other words, 'no gentlemen wanted',"
Bartescue chuckled. "Oh, well, I was only
teasing. I couldn't have gone anyway because
I tee off at one o'clock. I hope you have a
jolly hike," and with a wide, knowing grin,
the man bowed himself away.

"Do you think he suspected anything?" Bess asked in an undertone a moment later.

"He acted as if he did," Nancy said thoughtfully. "He seems to be watching us too, so we'll just walk off and not enter the woods until the coast is clear."

Soon Mortimer Bartescue grew tired of playing a waiting game and wandered into the hotel. With a careful glance about to make certain that they were seen by no other person, the girls cut through the dense timber and cautiously approached the old wooden bridge.

"The scarecrow is waving around as usual," Bess observed nervously as they glimpsed it through the trees. "I wonder if we'll hear that awful wailing noise again? If we do, I think I'll turn around and run straight back to the hotel."

" 'Fraidy cat," George teased.

"I rather hope we do hear it," Nancy remarked. "I'm sure there's a logical explanation for the sound if only we can find it."

"I'll gladly leave the job entirely to you," Bess said with a shiver. "I see no sense in coming here again, anyway."

"Didn't I find a treasure chest the last time?"

"Yes," Bess agreed soberly, "and that's all the more reason why we should stay away. I feel it in my bones that we're walking straight into trouble."

George and Nancy laughed at the girl's

fears, knowing that she was always inclined
to be timid. No unusual sound disturbed the
tranquility of the forest as they approached
the sagging bridge.

"This is the best place to cross the ravine, I
judge," Nancy declared as she glanced carefully up and down the stream. "I think the
bridge should bear our weight if we pass over
it one at a time."

She went on ahead, and after she had
reached the opposite side in safety, George
followed. Bess came last, uttering a muffled
little shriek as the flapping scarecrow caressed
her arm.

"Do control yourself, Bess," Nancy said severely. "We don't want to broadcast our arrival."

"You'd scream too if that thing wrapped
itself about your arm," Bess Fayne retorted.
"There's no one around here anyway."

"We can't be certain of that," Nancy replied, leading the way through the tangle of
bushes which lined the ravine.

"I can't see how you expect to find the
burned mansion when you don't know the
way," George complained as she ducked her
head to avoid being struck by a thorny branch.
"Did Sammy say it was on this side of the
bridge?"

"He pointed in this general direction. I
think we're heading right, for I see a trail."

Nancy indicated a faintly outlined path di-

rectly ahead. As the girls came up to it they
were a trifle puzzled to see still another trail
branching off away from the ravine.

"Which shall we take?" Bess inquired as
Nancy hesitated uncertainly. "It looks as if
the one which follows along the edge of the
ravine might have been used recently."

"Yes, but Sammy didn't indicate that the
old house lay in that direction. Let's try this
other trail first."

She pushed forward again, the scraggly
bushes tearing at her clothing. Bess and
George followed as best they could, but they
did not share their chum's enthusiasm for the
adventure.

"I've ruined my good dress," Bess complained crossly. "Is this trip worth it, I'd like
to know?"

Nancy merely laughed, refraining from telling the girls of her real purpose in wishing to
visit the burned mansion. She would have
liked to have taken Bess and George into her
confidence, but without her father's permission she was not free to divulge any of the
details of the jewel smuggling case. Presently
the three chums came to a clearing marked by
a high, uncut hedge.

"Thank goodness, we're out of the jungle at
last," Bess sighed wearily as she leaned
against a tree to rest. "Do you suppose this
is the estate, Nancy?"

"Yes, I can see something directly ahead

that looks like a building. This must have been a beautiful place when it was kept up."

The grounds covered an acre, and were wooded with giant oak and graceful willow trees. The yard had become choked with weeds, but the vestige of a rose garden remained. The green bushes had overgrown the rickety trellis which originally had supported them.

In the very center of the clearing was a huge pile of debris, from which there rose a charred pillar and several half-burned timbers. Little else remained of the once pretentious Judson mansion.

"Is this what we've come to see?" Bess asked in disappointment.

"I thought there would be more to it," Nancy admitted ruefully.

Just what she had expected to find the girl did not say. In her heart she had harbored a hope that the Judson fire had not been so devastating and might give up a clue, such as a photograph, which would identify a member of the family with the mysterious jeweled vanity case. Observing Nancy's look of disappointment, her chums shrewdly guessed that she had not told them everything.

"How did you know that a Judson family formerly lived here?" Bess asked curiously.

"Sammy was telling me. He said a young woman named Margaret who had had a very tragic life once resided in this house."

"I don't see how you hope to connect her with the jeweled vanity case," George said leadingly. "That's what you hope to do, isn't it?"

"Maybe," Nancy smiled impishly. "I really can't tell you anything about it just yet. I must have Dad's permission first."

"Oh, does this concern his case?" Bess asked in surprise.

"Don't ask me any more questions or I'll be telling everything I know—and that would never do. I can see there's nothing we can find here so let's start back to the hotel."

Bess and George did not urge their chum to reveal her secret, realizing that she had promised her father to remain silent. Few words were exchanged as the girls made their laborious way back to the ravine.

Nancy was absorbed with her own thoughts. Could Margaret Judson be the same sad, beautiful woman whom she had met at Hemlock Hall? The deduction seemed a reasonable one. It was possible also that the woman might be a member of an international jewel-theft gang.

"Yet if I am any judge of character she didn't look the type," Nancy reflected in bewilderment. "She appeared like a very fine woman who might have suffered intensely."

Her thoughts upon the subject ended abruptly at that point, for without warning a shrill scream broke upon the ears of the three startled girls. With one accord they halted, huddling together.

CHAPTER IX

A Mysterious Gardener

"THERE it is again!" Bess murmured apprehensively, clutching Nancy's hand. "The cry of the ghost!"

"The sound didn't seem to come from the direction of the bridge," George replied shakily, for she too had been frightened. "I thought it was almost like a scream."

The girls waited a moment, listening, but the cry was not repeated.

"I think it came from the golf course," George insisted. "Someone might have been struck with a ball."

Nancy did not express her opinion, although she disagreed with both her chums. She was certain that the locality was not haunted, and she felt equally sure that the cry had not been made by a person who had just been injured.

The girls went on and presently reached the dividing point of the two trails and Nancy's gaze roved down the path which led along the ravine.

"I think the sound came from that direction," she announced firmly. "Let's investigate——"

"Let's not," George cried, grasping her chum's arm. "We've had enough adventure for one day, Nancy Drew."

"Yes, you're altogether too daring," Bess added quickly. "I want to get away from this dreadful place before something happens."

Nancy's feeble protests were sternly overruled and she was fairly pulled along toward the haunted bridge. The girls darted across it and retraced their steps toward the golf course. To avoid meeting any players who might be coming down the fairway, they kept just within the fringe of woods. Now and then they could hear voices and knew that a match was being played somewhere near-by.

Suddenly a ball came whizzing through the air, striking a tree not more than a dozen yards from where the girls were walking. It bounced wickedly, coming to rest squarely behind another tree.

"Someone will have a mean shot to play," Nancy chuckled. "Let's duck back out of sight and watch."

Scarcely had the girls secreted themselves behind some trees when Mortimer Bartescue entered the woods. He was muttering to himself, savagely berating what he termed "his luck." The man hunted among the shrubbery for a few minutes and finally came upon his ball.

"Never mind, caddy," the girls heard him shout. "I've found it."

Satisfied that no one was near, Bartescue took

an iron club and deftly raked the ball from the hole in which it had lodged. Now, with it lying in an unobstructed path to the fairway, he played a clean shot out of the woods.

"Did you see that?" Nancy asked her companions in deep disgust. "He deliberately cheated."

"Someone should report such conduct," Bess declared angrily. "That man surely ought to be barred from competition."

"I should think his own conscience would plague him," George added. "But apparently nothing ever bothers him."

When the girls reached the hotel, they found Carson Drew sitting on the veranda. After chatting with the three for a few minutes he took Nancy aside and told her that he would have to leave for New York on the midnight train.

"Then shall I pack at once, Dad?"

"There is no necessity for ruining your vacation, Nancy. I expect to be gone only a short time. New York detectives have asked me to bring the carved chest and its contents there for examination."

"Then they think the jewelry may be stolen property?" Nancy asked quickly.

"Yes, the description tallies. While I am gone, Nancy, you might keep your eyes open for that woman you encountered at Hemlock Hall. In the light of recent developments she'll be wanted for questioning."

"I'll watch for her, Dad. I suspect that her name may be Margaret Judson but I have no proof."

"You've done remarkable work on the case so far," Mr. Drew praised his daughter warmly. "While I'm gone just be careful and remember that the woman we are after is a shrewd, dangerous individual."

"I'll bear that fact in mind," Nancy promised soberly.

She helped her father pack a light bag, and later that night went with him to the railroad station. Learning in the morning that her golf match would not be played until later in the day, Nancy set off alone for the nearby village, there to call upon her caddy's mother.

Mrs. Samuel Sutter Sr. was doing the family washing when the girl drove into the yard. The woman had been warned previously by her son of the impending visit, and greeted Nancy Drew cordially.

"I'm a sight in these old clothes," she apologized, jerking off a damp and soiled apron.

"I hope I'm not keeping you from your work," the girl said politely as she was escorted into the parlor.

"I was just hanging up the last basketful of wash when you drove in. No, I'm glad of a chance to sit down for a spell. I like nothing better than a good visit."

"Have you a large family, Mrs. Sutter?"

"Three boys," the woman replied proudly.

"Sammy, he's the middle one and the best worker of the lot. Many a day he brings two or three dollars home from the Deer Mountain golf course."

The loquacious mother launched into an account of the virtues of her various sons, so it was with difficulty that Nancy changed the subject to that of the Judson family.

"Oh, yes," said Mrs. Sutter with a nod, "Sammy was telling me you were interested in them, though I told him I didn't see why anyone would be about the Judson family. Aloof folks they were, never mixing with their neighbors. Margaret was a pretty girl but she aged up some after her parents both died. She was engaged to marry a college professor. I don't know what happened—some thought one thing, some another—but after the fire, she just up and ran off. I did washing for a woman who knew the young man. She told me he was all broke up over it and he never has married since."

"Why did Margaret run away?"

"Some folks said it was because she was so upset over her parents' death, and then the fire on top of it. Others thought maybe she just wanted to break the engagement and didn't have the courage to tell the professor."

"Is there no member of the Judson family living in the community now?"

"Oh, no, they're all dead except Miss Margaret and land knows whatever became of her. There's no one who even remembers the family very well except perhaps the old gardener."

Nancy had begun to fear that her trip to the Sutter home was entirely wasted, but at this last scrap of information she became alert again. Mrs. Sutter did not remember the man's name nor where he lived.

"I heard that for a while he sometimes would go back to the Judson place and cut the weeds, but I guess lately he's given up hope that Miss Margaret ever will come back."

"You have no idea where I can find this gardener, have you, Mrs. Sutter?"

"Not unless you happen to run into him by accident. He doesn't come to town very often, and I know of no one who could tell you where he lives."

"I'd give a great deal to find the man," Nancy murmured, thinking aloud.

"He couldn't tell you a bit more about the Judsons than I have," Mrs. Sutter said with a little toss of her head. "You're pretty interested in the family, aren't you?"

"Well, yes, I guess I am."

"No kin of yours, are they?"

"Not to my knowledge," Nancy answered, smiling. She could see that Mrs. Sutter was fairly overcome by curiosity. "I found something near the golf course which I thought might belong to Margaret Judson. For that reason I am trying to trace her."

The explanation partially satisfied Mrs. Sutter, and Nancy left before the woman could ask another question. In traveling back toward the Deer Mountain Hotel the girl stopped her car at a filling station, and learned from the attendant there that the old Judson estate could be reached by a dirt road which ran south of the ravine.

"I'll run out there just on the chance that the gardener may be somewhere about the premises," Nancy decided impulsively. "I'll still have time to get back to the hotel in time for my afternoon match."

The trip took a little over half an hour. Nancy left the car by the roadside and walked up an abandoned lane to the estate. At first she thought the place was deserted. Suddenly her heart leaped with hope as she glimpsed a man some distance away who was mowing weeds with a hand sickle.

"He must be the old gardener," she thought exultantly. "This is certainly my lucky day."

As she moved forward eagerly, the man looked up. Upon seeing her he dropped his sickle and started to run in the opposite direction.

"Wait!" Nancy called. "Please wait just a minute!"

If the gardener heard her he paid no heed. Leaping upon a bicycle which had been hidden in the bushes, he rode down a path and disappeared among the trees.

CHAPTER X

Nancy Accused

"Oh, don't run away!" Nancy shouted as she pursued the gardener. "I only want to talk with you."

The frightened man glanced over his shoulder, but instead of halting, peddled his bicycle all the faster. Breathless from running, the girl was compelled to abandon the chase. In deep chagrin she watched the man vanish into the woods.

"Now why did he act that way?" she speculated with a frown. "Perhaps he wasn't the gardener after all but some other person who had no right to be on the Judson property."

With a shrug she turned and made her way back to the automobile. At the hotel Bess and George were awaiting her on the veranda, and she could tell by the expressions on their faces that they had interesting information to impart.

"Mortimer Bartescue won his match yesterday," Bess announced as Nancy sat down beside her. "George and I took the liberty of asking the tournament chairman to see the score card."

"What did he have on number sixteen?" Nancy questioned curiously.

"A four. Imagine that!"

"He should have been disqualified for cheating. Did either of you speak to the chairman about it?"

"What would have been the use?" George asked wearily. "He would deny everything."

"Yes, that's true," Nancy admitted. "I guess it's better to overlook it, although Mr. Bartescue's opponent should have won the match."

"Bartescue was ahead before he came to the sixteenth hole," George revealed. "He didn't need to cheat to win, for the match already was his. He just couldn't bear to come in with a high score."

"It's disgusting," Nancy murmured. "I wonder how the other matches are turning out? Let's walk down toward the sixteenth and watch some of the players."

"The fairway along the woods is always a critical place," Bess added as the girls arose. "Many a match has been lost on that hole."

They sauntered along, pausing at the seventeenth green to watch two players hole their putts, and then moved on toward the woods.

"Isn't that Sammy Sutter?" Nancy asked presently, indicating a boy who could be seen just within the fringe of timber. "I do believe he intends to hunt for my lost golf ball."

"He's peering into the woods at the identical

place where your ball went in," Bess agreed. "Sammy said he wouldn't go near the haunted bridge for a million dollars."

"I tried to convince him that the spot wasn't haunted," Nancy said with a chuckle. "I'm not certain that I succeeded."

It was obvious to the watchers that the caddy feared to enter the woods. He seemed to be having a mental struggle with himself. Finally gaining temporary mastery over his misgivings, he disappeared from view. The girls quickened their steps.

"Let's have a little fun," Nancy laughed.

Unable to resist the temptation, she gave a low, moaning wail, throwing her voice so that it seemed to come from the direction of the haunted bridge.

The effect was astounding. Sammy uttered a wild shriek and came plunging out of the woods. He stopped short upon seeing Nancy and her chums, and a flush overspread his freckled face.

"Oh—" he stammered in confusion—"I thought——"

"That the ghost was talking again?" Nancy supplied, smiling. "No, we were just playing a little joke on you, Sammy."

"I guess I'm silly to be scared," the boy admitted, hanging his head.

"Everyone has fears of one kind or another," Nancy said kindly. "By the way, Sammy, I'm depending upon you to caddy for me this afternoon."

"I'll be ready whenever you say, Miss Drew."

"Then be at the first tee by two-thirty. Our match will be a hard one."

"You'll win," the boy said confidently, "and I'll be pulling for you all the way."

The girls chatted with Sammy for a few minutes. Then, leaving him to search for the autographed golf ball, they walked back to the hotel for luncheon.

In passing through the lobby Nancy saw a letter in her room mailbox. Thinking that it might be a communication from her father, she stopped to ask the clerk for it.

"Oh, it can't be from him," she observed in disappointment as she studied the handwriting.

"I'll venture it's a note from your new admirer," Bess declared teasingly.

The letter was indeed from Mortimer Bartescue. He wished Nancy luck in her afternoon match, offering the information that he had defeated his opponent by an easy margin.

"If you win today, we shall have to celebrate our joint victory," he wrote. "I shall look forward to escorting you to the dance at Hemlock Hall."

"The conceit of the man!" Nancy fumed as she read the note. "He seems to take it for granted that I'll be thrilled to go."

"I'd turn him down in no uncertain terms," Bess declared.

"I think perhaps I'll go," Nancy said slowly.

Bess and George stared in bewilderment.

"Oh, not because I like the man! I detest him, but I have a great desire to attend a dance at Hemlock Hall, and unfortunately one needs an escort."

"I don't see how you could expect to have any fun with that man," George said discouragingly.

"I'd not be going for the fun of it. My purpose would be to study the guests—investigation work for my father."

"Oh, that's different," Bess answered in relief. "By the way, two boys here at the hotel have asked George and me to the same dance."

"Did you say you would go?"

"We haven't promised yet," Bess replied, "but if you want to go with Mortimer Bartescue we could accept and all keep together."

"All right," Nancy agreed after a moment's thought. "I'll tell Mr. Bartescue I'll attend the dance. And now, let's have luncheon for it will soon be time for me to play my match."

When the girls later came from the dining room, the hotel clerk signaled to them, revealing that another communication had arrived for Nancy. This time it was a message from Mr. Drew. The lawyer had wired that he wished his daughter to meet him at the station early the next morning. The jewelry contained in the carved chest had been examined and he emphasized the need of locating the owner of the jeweled vanity case immediately.

"There's a chance I may see Margaret Judson at the dance tonight," Nancy thought as she read the message a second time. "For once Mortimer Bartescue has actually done me a favor."

It was after two o'clock as the girls walked to the first tee, and Nancy resolutely put aside all thoughts of the baffling mystery. Her opponent, a stout, muscular woman, nodded curtly as she tested out her swing.

"This will be no friendly match," Nancy decided shrewdly. "Miss Allison is out to win at any price."

They halved the first three holes as neither player seemed able to gain the advantage. Nancy was conscious that the other woman watched every shot like a hawk, hoping to trip up her opponent on some technical point of the game. Accordingly, the girl was very careful never to do anything which might be questioned.

Nancy's hand pained her a great deal, but she made no mention of the handicap under which she was playing. At first she was able to pound out long, straight balls, but gradually she grew weary and found herself in one difficulty after another.

Miss Allison won two holes in succession, and a look of smug satisfaction came over her face. It faded away when Nancy, fighting gamely, took the next hole, halved the following and then won again to square the match.

At the sixteenth tee the match was still even, although Miss Allison held the honor of driving off first. She sent a long ball safely past the woods and then it was Nancy's turn.

As the girl took a back swing with her club, she let her mind wander momentarily. She began thinking about her father and the jewel-thief mystery in which he was so deeply interested, with the result that her ball sliced wickedly, and to the horror of Sammy it entered the woods.

"Oh, too bad," said Miss Allison with a false show of sympathy. "I'm afraid that will put you out of the match."

"Perhaps not," Nancy said cheerfully. "There are still a few holes to play."

Summoning his courage, Sammy plunged into the woods, locating the ball in a deep hole by a tree.

"It's almost unplayable," he told Nancy with a groan.

Without a word she asked for her mashie and struck the ball with all her strength. The shot was a remarkable one, and the ball sailed cleanly out of the woods. Even so, at the end of the hole it was found that Nancy had taken one more stroke than had her opponent.

"I am afraid this is very nearly the end," Nancy said cheerfully as they walked to the next tee. "I am one down now, and—" She started to add that her hand was paining her dreadfully, but quickly broke off.

She had no intention of giving up easily, and managed to tie Miss Allison on the seventeenth.

As they played toward the last green, she put all her strength into each shot, wincing with pain each time.

"A tie isn't enough here," she said grimly to herself. "I must win by a stroke or I'll lose the match and be out of the tournament!"

A little crowd had gathered by the green to watch the players come in. Miss Allison, with victory so near, became excited and made a wild putt. Nancy then calmly dropped her ball into the cup, tying the match again.

According to the rules, an extra hole must be played. As the two went back to the first tee the crowd followed. An audience seemed to bother Miss Allison. Her drive was short, and her next shot went into the rough. She lost the hole by two strokes, and it was Nancy's match!

Instead of offering congratulations, Miss Allison turned on her heel and walked away angrily. She was seen to enter the golf house office.

"Oh, you were splendid, Nancy!" Bess praised her friend gleefully, while George gave her chum a hearty hug. "Miss Allison wasn't a very good sport, was she?"

"Her heart was set upon winning all right."

Blissfully unaware that Miss Allison had issued a complaint against Nancy, the girls walked slowly away from the golf course. A man came toward them from the office, and they could see by the expression on his face that something was amiss.

"Miss Drew, will you come with me, please?" he requested quietly. "There seems to be a little misunderstanding."

"Misunderstanding?" Nancy echoed in astonishment as she followed the man.

"Your opponent claims the match."

"Why, I won it fairly on the nineteenth hole," Nancy replied with justifiable indignation. "There were many witnesses, too."

"Miss Allison claims the match on account of the sixteenth hole," the man told her gravely. "She says that you moved your ball after it went into the woods."

CHAPTER XI

The Crumpled Telegram

Nancy was stunned completely by the false accusation.

"Why, how can you say such a thing?" she demanded angrily of Miss Allison. "You know it isn't true."

"It certainly is," the woman retorted, whirling about. "I am sure you moved your ball for otherwise you never could have reached the fairway. I distinctly heard your caddy tell you that the shot was unplayable."

"Nevertheless, I made it, and Sammy will tell you so!"

"I put no trust in a caddy's word."

"If you were so certain I cheated why didn't you speak of it at the time?" Nancy asked sharply. "You seemed well enough satisfied when you won the hole."

Bess and George had followed their chum to the golf office. Unable to remain quiet, they flew to her defense.

"Nancy has never cheated in all her life!" George insisted angrily. "You're just provoked because she defeated you!"

The tournament chairman looked nervous and worried.

"Now, let's be calm about this," he said anxiously. "We'll try to decide this matter fairly——"

"The match is clearly mine," Miss Allison snapped. "Miss Drew cheated."

"Here, here, what's the trouble?" asked a masculine voice from behind.

The girls turned to see Mortimer Bartescue standing in the doorway. He repeated his question and the tournament chairman reluctantly explained the difficulty.

"Why, Miss Allison's accusation is entirely false," the man responded officiously. "It so happened that I was walking along the woods as the match was being played. I saw Miss Drew drive into the trees, and I watched her execute her shot. It was a beauty."

"Oh, thank you," Nancy gasped gratefully, and for the first time since arriving at Deer Mountain Hotel she decided that Mortimer Bartescue had his good points.

"If everyone defends Miss Drew I may as well drop the charge!" Miss Allison said angrily as she walked from the office. She cast a look of hatred at Mortimer Bartescue and added, "However, I don't believe that you were even near the woods!"

Nancy glanced quickly at the man but his face was mask-like in its lack of expression. Had he deliberately lied in order to help her? She could not be certain, but at any rate her conscience was clear for she knew that she had won the match honestly.

"Don't mind Miss Allison," the tournament chairman said to Nancy after the woman had gone. "She always loses hard."

"Then the charges will be dropped?"

"Certainly. If she had any grievance she should have made it known before the next holes were played. I am sorry you were embarrassed, Miss Drew."

Mortimer Bartescue followed the girls from the office, smirking with pleasure.

"Did you really see me play my shot?" Nancy inquired gravely of the man.

"Why certainly," he returned, his eyes twinkling. "Didn't you see me there in the woods?"

"No, I didn't."

"Well, you must have been looking the wrong way then. By the way, did you receive my note?"

"Yes," Nancy admitted reluctantly.

She was half inclined to say that she could not attend the dance, yet she did not wish to turn down an invitation to Hemlock Hall. Hiding her dislike for the man, she politely accepted his invitation to go with him that evening.

Nancy could not rid herself of the conviction that Bartescue had lied about being in the woods. Later in the afternoon she made it her purpose to inquire if anyone had seen the man at the time the match was being played. She was not surprised when a boy at the soda fountain recalled that Bartescue had spent nearly an hour in the hotel drug store between the hours of four and five.

"Mr. Bartescue told me not to tell anyone," the boy grinned, "but I didn't promise to keep quiet about it. He wrote out a telegram while he was having his soda."

Nancy waited eagerly, hoping that the boy who so much enjoyed imparting information would tell more. She was not disappointed.

"He wrote out two or three telegrams but couldn't seem to get one that suited him. He left one wadded up on the counter and I read it."

"You did?"

"Sure, see, here it is." The boy took a crumpled paper from his pocket and waved it before Nancy's eyes.

She was able to make out two words in the quick glance permitted her; the name of Margaret Judson.

"Want to read it?" the boy invited.

Nancy was sorely tempted, but she shook her head.

"No, I'm not interested in Mr. Bartescue's private affairs."

The boy thrust the paper into his pocket again and a moment later was called away to wait on another customer. Nancy left the shop.

She sought her chums, wondering if she had made a mistake in declining to read the telegram. What connection could this Mortimer Bartescue have with Margaret Judson? Neither Bess nor George could offer a theory although they were deeply interested to learn that the man had intended to communicate with her by wire.

"I caught only a glimpse of the writing," Nancy told her chums, "but I'm sure it wasn't the same as those other samples of Mr. Bartescue's hand."

"Perhaps tonight you can induce him to write on your dance program," Bess suggested thoughtfully.

"I might try," Nancy agreed, "but I judge he'll be too shrewd to do so."

"You want to be careful tonight," George warned, looking worried. "If Mr. Bartescue should be an underworld character——."

"I mean to use caution," Nancy returned, "and I have a request to make. We leave the hotel at eight o'clock. I'd like to have you girls and your escorts follow closely in your car."

"We'll do our best to keep you in sight," Bess promised. "Then if anything should go wrong, you could just yell and we'd come dashing to the rescue."

"I trust there will be no need to send out an S.O.S. call," Nancy laughed.

Shortly before eight o'clock the boys who were to escort Bess and George arrived in their

car. Nancy was worried for fear Mortimer
Bartescue would ruin her plans by being late,
but to her relief he appeared within a few minutes. As he assisted her into a high-powered
touring car, Nancy glimpsed her chums and
their escorts in a nearby automobile, waiting
to follow. For a time her companion drove at
a moderate pace, but when the road straight-
ened out he speeded up until the other car was
left far behind.

"Oh, let's not go so fast!" Nancy protested
anxiously.

"We're only doing seventy," Bartescue told
her, stepping even harder on the gasoline pedal.
"This is the way I like to travel."

"Well, I don't. If you refuse to slow down
I'll never go with you anywhere again."

"Oh, all right," the man grumbled, grudg-
ingly reducing the speed of the car.

After that he drove at a moderate pace.
However, in glancing back Nancy was troubled
to observe that the car in which her chums were
traveling had been lost to view.

"What's the matter with you tonight anyway?" Bartescue demanded gruffly. "You act
nervous."

"If I am it was your driving that made me
so," Nancy answered a trifle irritably.

For some minutes they drove in silence. The
girl was wondering if she dared broach the
subject of the day's golf match. Finally, with
an attempt at tact, she suggested to her escort

that she felt he had told an untruth about seeing her play from the woods solely because he
meant to be chivalrous.

"I guess maybe that was the way of it,"
Bartescue admitted with a chuckle. "Did you
really cheat?"

"Certainly not!"

"Now don't get huffy," her companion said
quickly. "It wouldn't make any difference to
me if you did or if you didn't."

Nancy had all she could do to control her
temper, but she kept telling herself over and
over that she would gain nothing by revealing
her true feelings. Taking a different tack, she
flattered her escort a bit, and when he was in a
pleasant mood casually asked him if he knew
Miss Judson.

"Margaret Judson?" the man inquired indifferently. "Oh, I met her in Europe years ago.
A pretty woman, but boring."

"Where is she living at the present time?"

"I don't feel at liberty to tell you, Miss Drew.
I happen to know that she doesn't wish her
whereabouts to be revealed."

"I rather thought she might be living near
here," Nancy said, watching her companion
closely.

"Perhaps she is," Bartescue smiled.

Another silence fell upon the pair, which was
not broken until Hemlock Hall was reached.
Nancy loitered as long as she dared in the dressing room, studying the various women who

came and went. She was greatly relieved when Bess and George arrived, and they too were overjoyed for they had feared that their chum might be in need of aid.

"Try not to lose our car going back to our hotel," Nancy urged as she parted company with them. "In the meantime you might keep your eyes open for a woman with a jeweled vanity case. If you should see one, report to me instantly."

Mortimer Bartescue was provoked because his partner had remained so long in the dressing room, and his irritation grew as the dance progressed. He had intended to have the girl entirely to himself, but many young men cut in upon their dances together; they would scarcely take a turn about the floor before someone would tap him on the shoulder. However, in a few minutes she would be claimed again by the man who had brought her.

The music was excellent, but Nancy did not enjoy dancing with Bartescue. Finally she offered an excuse for escaping to the dressing room and there maintained an alert watch for a woman with a jeweled vanity case.

"This night will be entirely wasted, I'm afraid," she thought in disappointment. "Miss Judson isn't here, and it begins to look as if I'll not find a single clue which will help my father's case."

Nancy reluctantly went back to dance once more with her escort. Presently, when he absented himself from her side for a moment, she wandered into a small parlor adjoining the ballroom. The place was vacant. She turned to leave, only to halt as she heard a low murmur of voices.

Two women were sitting on the porch and conversing earnestly. Through the open window their words reached Nancy clearly.

"But I tell you I have no money to give you for the vanity case," the one said in a harassed tone. "Please try to understand."

"How do I know you didn't sell it?" the other asked harshly.

The women lowered their voices so Nancy was unable to hear anything more. She moved swiftly toward the window.

Apparently the two heard someone coming, for they quickly arose and moved away, walking hurriedly toward the garden. The porch was dark. Nancy could not see the face of either woman but she observed that one was dressed in a flowered silk gown which hung in long, loose folds.

"I must learn who they are," Nancy thought excitedly. "One of those women may be Margaret Judson!"

CHAPTER XII

A Clue from the Caddy

By the time Nancy had managed to unfasten the door and step out on the porch, the two women had vanished. She ran down the steps into the garden, satisfied that they had taken one of the many winding paths leading from the hotel.

A number of couples were enjoying the moonlight, some idling near the fountains, others walking slowly up and down as they listened to the strains of the dance orchestra. Nancy darted here and there, searching frantically for the woman in the flowered dress.

Suddenly, far ahead of her, she thought she saw the person she was seeking. In her eagerness to reach the woman before she should disappear again, the girl rushed blindly forward, running full-tilt into a couple who were spending their honeymoon at the hotel. The startled young husband, just in the act of bestowing a tender kiss upon his bride, was nearly thrown off balance.

"Oh, I beg your pardon," Nancy stammered, backing away in embarrassment.

Taking another path, the girl continued her search for the woman in flowered silk, but she was nowhere to be found. At length Nancy went back into the hotel and mingled with the guests in the lobby. There her efforts were rewarded, for she saw a woman in a flowered gown enter an elevator.

Nancy was too late to catch the same lift but she raced upstairs, reaching the next floor just as the elevator halted there. The lady who alighted was not the person she thought to be Margaret Judson. The girl hesitated; then, deciding to take a chance, she said quickly:

"I beg your pardon, but do you know where Miss Judson is?"

The woman in question gazed at the speaker in surprise but replied evenly:

"Probably she has gone to her room."

Nancy could not prolong the conversation, so she was compelled to allow the woman to pass on down the hall. Highly jubilant over the information she had gleaned, the girl hurried downstairs to consult the desk clerk.

"I understand that a Miss Judson is staying here," she said. "Will you please give me the number of her room?"

The man consulted a book which lay on the desk.

"The woman has just checked out," he reported.

"Oh, are you sure?" Nancy gasped in disappointment.

"Quite sure. She left about ten minutes ago."

"Can you give me her forwarding address?"

"She left none."

As Nancy was recovering from her disappointment, Mortimer Bartescue sauntered into the lobby.

"Oh, here you are, Miss Drew," he said with a trace of unpleasantness. "You don't seem to care for dancing this evening."

"I didn't mean to run off," Nancy apologized quickly. "You see, I thought I saw Miss Judson here in the lobby and I wanted to speak with her. Tell me, have you seen her tonight?"

"Perhaps," the man answered with a mysterious smile. "Remember what I told you in the car?"

"You mean about her not wishing to have her whereabouts known?"

"That's right. Now just forget all about Miss Judson and we'll enjoy this next waltz together."

Against her will Nancy was led back to the ballroom. She did not try to escape from her escort again. Shortly before the last dance, however, she found an opportunity to speak with her chums, requesting them once more to follow closely in their car during the ride back to the Deer Mountain Hotel.

Despite Nancy's fears, the homeward drive proved to be uneventful. She tumbled into bed at a late hour, tired and more than half con-

vinced that the efforts of the evening had been
futile. It occurred to her to wonder if Mortimer
Bartescue had gone to the dance for the deliber-
ate purpose of meeting Margaret Judson, but
the thought was put aside quickly. She fell into
a troubled sleep, to be awakened by the alarm
at six.

"Who left that clock turned on?" Nancy
moaned drowsily. Then she remembered that
she had set it herself. Soon it would be time for
her to meet her father at the railroad station.

Giving herself fifteen minutes in which to
dress, Nancy snatched a cup of coffee at the
hotel cafe and then was off to meet the train.
By seven o'clock father and daughter were
seated opposite each other at a table in the
station lunchroom.

"Did you have a successful trip, Dad?" the
girl asked as soon as they had given their breakfast order. "What did you learn about the
contents of the carved chest?"

"Here is a bit of information which may surprise you, Nancy. Only one article in the entire
collection proved to be stolen property."

"And I'd say that is the jeweled vanity
case."

"Yes. The other articles could not be identified. Of course, they may have been stolen in
this country very recently. At any rate, the
jewelry, with the exception of the vanity case,
does not belong to the cache known to be held
by the gang of international smugglers."

Nancy listened to a more detailed account of her father's visit to New York, whereupon she in turn told him of her own activities during his absence.

"I was sure I had located Miss Judson at Hemlock Hall," she finished apologetically. "Unfortunately, she got away before I could talk to her."

"We must bend all our energies toward tracing her," Mr. Drew said soberly. "From the clues you have gathered I feel certain she's the person we are after."

The lawyer wished to drive without delay to Hemlock Hall, and Nancy was very glad to accompany him. However, the trip proved to be a wasted one. Although they inquired at the railroad station and various garages and other likely places, no one could offer the slightest information as to where Miss Judson had gone.

Mr. Drew and Nancy were compelled to hurry back to the Deer Mountain Hotel directly after luncheon, for the girl was scheduled to play in the semi-finals of the golf tournament at two o'clock. As usual, Sammy served as her caddy.

The match was a close one, but Nancy played an excellent game, scarcely noticing the pain in her hand. To the delight of her chums she won on the fifteenth hole. As she finished out the round so that she might turn in a complete score, she jokingly asked Sammy if he had found her Jimmy Harlow ball.

"I think I'll never find it now," he told her

gloomily. "Maybe someone else picked it up."

"Have you noticed anyone searching in the woods by the bridge?" Nancy inquired alertly.

"This morning I saw an old man with a stick poking around in the mud by the bank of the stream."

Nancy pressed the lad for a more detailed description of the person in question, but he was unable to give it. The girl said no more, but as she walked slowly back to the hotel she reflected that Sammy unknowingly had offered her a clue which was worth investigating.

"That old man may have been the Judson gardener," she thought, "or possibly he was someone searching for the carved chest which I found buried in the mud bank."

Nancy was afraid that it might be too late to find the man, but she decided to make another visit to the haunted bridge immediately. Bess and George were very glad to accompany her, so the three girls set off across the golf course. They had gone only a few steps when Bess stopped short.

"Here comes that pest, Mortimer Bartescue!" she exclaimed in an undertone. "Now what shall we do?"

CHAPTER XIII

A Telltale Photograph

Thinking very quickly, Nancy greeted the newcomer with a warm smile, asking innocently:

"Oh, Mr. Bartescue, did my father see you this afternoon?"

"Why no," the man answered in surprise, falling into the trap. "Did he wish to speak with me?"

"Well, I heard him say he was looking for a tennis partner. Dad is remarkably good at the game."

Upon many an occasion Mortimer Bartescue had boasted to Nancy that he excelled in the sport; in fact, according to his own story, he was an expert swimmer, a good skater, a superior marksman and a fine rider. Tennis and golf, however, he claimed as his pet hobbies.

"I see my father on the veranda!" Nancy cried. Waving to her parent, she motioned for him to join the group.

"Dad, I've found a wonderful tennis partner for you," she declared as he came up.

He suspected that Nancy wished to rid herself of Mr. Bartescue. While he disliked the man heartily, he was rather curious to test out the fellow's skill as a tennis player.

Mr. Drew and Mortimer Bartescue sought the courts and the girls made their way toward the haunted bridge. Dark clouds were moving swiftly overhead, and by the time the chums reached the woods a strong wind was blowing.

"Do you think it will rain soon?" Bess asked anxiously, scanning the sky overhead.

"Oh, not for an hour at least," Nancy replied carelessly. "Even if it should, we'll be partially protected by trees. Let's not turn back now."

The girls struck off through the timber, and soon were within view of the old bridge. With the sun under a cloud it was dark and gloomy beneath the canopy of trees. Bess shivered and kept close to her companions. Suddenly they were startled to hear the same groaning sound which had frightened them on their previous visit.

"Oh!" Bess squealed in terror, clutching George's arm. "There it is again!"

Nancy warned her to be quiet, and for several minutes the girls stood perfectly still, waiting for the sound to be repeated. No one could be seen anywhere near the bridge.

"I believe the noise came from far down the ravine," Nancy whispered after she was convinced that the groan would not be repeated. "Come on, let's investigate."

After briefly searching the locality near the

bridge, the girls turned their attention to the trail which had interested them upon their first visit to the spot. Footprints were plainly visible. Nancy wondered if someone had not used the path within the past twenty-four hours.

"Let's not go that way today," Bess pleaded, reading her chum's thoughts. "It's growing darker every instant, and we don't want to be caught in a storm."

Scarcely had the words been spoken when a shrill scream broke the stillness of the forest. This time Nancy was certain that the cry had come from far down the ravine.

"Come on!" she urged excitedly. "We'll solve this old mystery yet!"

She darted forward down the path, oblivious of the thorny bushes which tore at her hair and clothing. George and Bess followed as best they could, though with no zest for an adventure which might lead them straight into trouble.

Suddenly Nancy halted. A short distance ahead in a tiny clearing she beheld a log cabin. Smoke was curling lazily from the chimney.

"I didn't know anyone lived here in the woods," Bess gasped in surprise as she too observed the dwelling. "The scream seemed to come from that direction, too."

"Yes," Nancy answered in a whisper.

She was debating what course of action to follow, when the cabin door opened suddenly and an old man carrying a rifle was seen to emerge. The girls shrank back deeper into the

woods, fearing for a moment that their presence
in the locality was known to the stranger. But
as he gazed meditatively up at the sky, they
decided that he could not have seen them.

"It's the same old fellow who was working
near the Judson property," Nancy whispered
to her chums. "I believe he must be the gardener."

She was tempted to step forward and accost
him, but recalling how he had run away in fright
the previous day, she bided her time.

"Let's watch and see what he intends to do
with that rifle," she warned her companions.

The old man shouldered his gun, and without
glancing toward the woods where the girls were
sheltered, struck off in the general direction of
the Judson mansion.

"I believe he's only going hunting," George
declared. "Probably he is after squirrels."

Cautiously the girls followed. Suddenly Bess
tripped over a mossy log and as she fell head-
long in the trail, gave a faint outcry. The man
with the rifle immediately halted and glanced
back. Nancy and her chums crouched low.

Apparently satisfied that the sound he had
heard was made by some wild animal, the
hunter slowly walked on again. Presently,
sighting a squirrel in a nearby tree, he swiftly
raised his weapon to his shoulder and took careful aim.

There came a loud explosion as he pulled the
trigger, and the girls saw a sudden flash of fire.

They gasped in horror for obviously something had gone wrong. The man uttered a sharp moan of pain and staggered backward, collapsing on the ground.

"He's hurt!" Nancy cried. Forgetting everything else, she darted from her hiding place.

The victim did not stir as the girls reached his side, and for a moment they feared that he was dead. However, as Nancy bent anxiously over him she was relieved to see that he still breathed. A slight trickle of blood oozed from a wound in his forehead.

"We must get the man back to the cabin," Nancy told her chums.

Although the gardener was slightly built, the girls found themselves heavily taxed to carry him even the short distance to the clearing. He moaned several times, murmuring a name which they were unable to distinguish.

The girls laid the wounded man gently on a bed and Bess looked about in search of water. The bucket by the stove was empty, but remembering that she had noticed a well outside, she hastened to fill the container.

George and Nancy worked over the unconscious man, bathing his bruised forehead and applying cold compresses to his temples, yet their best efforts failed to arouse him.

"I don't know what more to do," Nancy admitted in desperation. "George, we must go for a doctor at once."

CHAPTER XIV

A Mystery Explained

"Let me run back to the hotel," George said quickly. "I'd rather do that than stay here— I feel so useless just looking at that poor man and knowing there's nothing I can do for him."

"You're not afraid to cross the haunted bridge alone?" Nancy asked quietly.

George hesitated, then shook her head. With a storm brewing the forest would be black as night. Of course she would be nervous, but with a man's life in jeopardy she must put aside her own fears.

"Shall I go with you?" Bess offered.

"No, stay with Nancy. She may need your help. I'll hurry as fast as I can."

Nancy took an old coat from a nail on the wall and flung it over George's shoulders.

"Wear this," she advised. "When the rain falls it will be a regular downpour."

George nodded grimly, and buttoning the coat about her she hurried from the cabin. A cool breeze struck her face. She knew that the storm could not be far away.

"I hate to see her start off alone," Nancy murmured anxiously as she watched from the window, "but I feel confident she'll make it."

When George was out of sight the other girls returned to the bedside of the old man. He was tossing about restlessly and they tried their best to soothe him.

"You are good," he whispered once as Nancy held his hand. "You are kind."

Presently there came the loud patter of raindrops on the roof. Nancy arose to close the windows. One of the sashes stuck fast so she looked about the kitchen for a tool with which to loosen it.

Opening a drawer of the high cupboard, she was amazed to come upon an assortment of papers. Thinking that she might find a letter which would serve to identify the unconscious man, Nancy swiftly examined the documents. Unexpectedly her hand encountered a faded photograph which had been kept between two sheets of stiff cardboard.

The picture, taken at a studio, was the likeness of a beautiful young girl. Nancy stared at the photograph and her heart leaped high. Across the bottom of the picture in a bold scrawl were the words:

"To my faithful friend Joe Haley—Margaret Judson."

Nancy's gaze went swiftly to the man who lay motionless on the bed by the window. Was he Joe Haley and was Joe Haley the Judson gardener?

"The girl of this picture is the person I met,

in the powder room at Hemlock Hall!'' she told herself. ''My theory regarding her identity was correct.''

Nancy studied the photograph for several minutes, reflecting that it must have been taken in the days before Margaret Judson's life had become burdened with trouble.

''This man probably is Joe Haley and the one person who would know where the woman lives,'' she thought. ''He should be able to tell me a great deal about her—if only he regains consciousness again.''

''Nancy, aren't you going to close that window?'' Bess broke in upon her reflections. ''The wind is blowing directly across the bed.''

''I'll have it down in a jiffy, Bess.''

Slipping the photograph into the front of her dress, Nancy found an implement and soon had the window closed. Before she could turn aside, a streak of lightning had flashed across the sky. At the same moment the girls heard a wild cry which seemed to issue from a point only a few yards back of the cabin.

''What was that?'' Bess cried in terror, springing up from her chair.

''I mean to find out,'' Nancy said grimly, flinging open the cabin door.

''Don't leave me here alone,'' Bess pleaded, but her words fell upon deaf ears.

Nancy darted out into the rain, determined to learn the cause of the weird scream. She moved swiftly toward the rear of the cabin, feeling certain that the cry had come from that direction.

She glanced quickly about but could see no one in the clearing. Just beyond stretched the woods, and as the girl gazed toward it she caught the gleam of wire mesh netting through the trees.

"What can that be?" she asked herself, and fearlessly moved toward the forest.

As she drew closer she saw that the wire netting comprised a series of cages. Nancy's amazement grew as she observed that the enclosures contained wild animals. There were several rabbits, some foxes and one wolf, while in a particularly strong cage, set up some distance from the others, was a chained young mountain lion. As the girl cautiously approached, the animal threw back its shapely head and gave a scream which would chill the blood of any listener.

Disturbed by the storm, the animals were scurrying about in their pens. Nancy wondered if the pets belonged to Joe Haley, but there was no opportunity to investigate further for the rain was falling steadily. Not caring to get drenched, she turned and fled back toward the cabin.

Midway across the clearing Nancy heard her name called. Bess appeared in the doorway, motioning frantically.

"Nancy! Nancy!" she called in distressed tones. "Come here quickly!"

CHAPTER XV

RAMBLING WORDS

NANCY reached her chum's side, thoroughly drenched and quite breathless from running.

"What is it, Bess?" she asked anxiously, grasping the girl's trembling arm. "Is the patient worse?"

"No, he's just the same."

"Then what is wrong? Why did you call?"

"I was frightened," Bess admitted ruefully. "I heard that dreadful scream again. I'm afraid to have you go into the woods alone. Something terrible might happen to you."

Nancy was so relieved at her chum's words that it was difficult for her not to laugh.

"There's nothing to fear, Bess. Those strange sounds we've been hearing are made by wild animals—pets that are kept in cages back of this cabin."

"Wild animals?" Bess asked in a quavering voice.

"Yes, I suspect they are the gardener's pets. The scream you just heard was made by a young mountain lion."

Bess still looked unconvinced and Nancy

promised to show her the cages as soon as the rain slackened.

"I don't want to go near the place," Bess said with a shiver. "I can't for the life of me see why anyone would keep wild animals on the place."

Nancy went inside the cabin to sit at the bedside of the wounded man. There seemed to be no change in his condition. She wished that George would hurry back with the doctor. Presently the rain slackened and the girl began to move restlessly about the room.

"There's nothing I can do here until the doctor comes," she said to Bess. "If you're not afraid to stay alone I believe I'll go outside and look around again."

Walking back of the cabin, Nancy gazed about the premises with a critical eye. The little plot of ground was well tended, with flower-beds banked against either side of the building. To the right was a garden of vegetables, and as the girl paused to glance at it she noticed many unfamiliar plants. Near by stood an improvised hot-house made from old window glass, and Nancy felt certain that many of the plants contained beneath it were rare tropical specimens.

"Why, I believe Mr. Haley must be a naturalist," she thought in some surprise. "He seems to have a keen interest in both botany and zoology."

Convinced that the injured man was no or.

dinary gardener, Nancy wandered back to the cabin. Bess was relieved to see her arrive, for old Mr. Haley had begun to toss restlessly on his pillow. It was with increasing difficulty that she restrained him.

As Nancy seated herself at the bedside, the old man rolled over and muttered a few words. She bent closer in an effort to distinguish what he was saying.

"He murmured something about a 'Miss Margaret' a moment ago," Bess told her chum in a whisper. "I couldn't make out anything but the name."

For several minutes the patient lay perfectly still. Then his eyelids fluttered open and he mumbled:

"Please, Miss Margaret—don't stay away. I can't find it—I've tried, but I can't." His words ended in an incoherent mumble. A moment later, apparently under the impression that the pet mountain lion was creating another disturbance, he said in a clear, stern voice:

"Oh, you bad pussy, don't scream so!"

"The poor fellow," Bess murmured to her chum, "he's completely out of his head. What do you suppose it is that he has been trying to find?"

Nancy shook her head as she applied another cold cloth to the man's brow. She was desperately afraid that he might never recover, in which event he could not help clear up the mystery surrounding Margaret Judson. It seemed to her that George was taking a great deal of time to make the trip back to the Deer Mountain Hotel. She wished now that she had gone herself.

"What was that?" Bess cried hopefully, springing up from her chair by the window. "I thought I heard voices in the woods."

Nancy flung open the cabin door, staring in astonished delight as she saw six persons emerge from among the trees. George and an elderly man whom the girls recognized as Doctor Aikerman were in the lead, and directly behind trooped Carson Drew, Ned Nickerson and two strange youths.

"We'll have plenty of help now, thank goodness," she gasped. "Ned and his friends must have arrived at the hotel earlier than they expected!"

Nancy led Doctor Aikerman to the bedside of the patient whom he said he did not know. While he was making his examination the girl had an opportunity to meet Ned's college friends, Bud Mason and Bill Cowan.

"We had just reached the hotel when George came dashing up to tell your father you were in need of help out here," Ned explained. "We all jumped into my car, and after driving as far as we could we cut across the woods."

"May I have some boiling water?" the physician requested at that moment, and Nancy flew to get it for him.

"Is the man badly injured?" she inquired

anxiously as she watched the doctor work over the patient.

"H-m, can't tell yet," he murmured without glancing up. "There seems to be a piece of shell imbedded in his forehead. Will you take these instruments and boil them for me, please?"

As it became evident to the others that the doctor meant to remove the shell, they hastily retreated from the cabin. Nancy alone remained to assist the man of medicine.

"Have you a steady nerve?" he questioned her.

"I think so," Nancy answered quietly.

The operation was not a pleasant thing to witness, but at last it was finished, and the doctor declared that the patient had an excellent chance to recover.

"Have you ever studied nursing?" he asked Nancy abruptly.

"Oh, no, I've had only training in first aid."

"You seem to have missed your calling," the doctor told her with a smile. "You appear to have a natural bent for nursing."

Nancy flushed at the praise. After helping the physician gather up his instruments she went outside to inform her father and the others that the operation was over.

"Would you consider it advisable to transfer the patient to a hospital?" Carson Drew presently asked the doctor. "I'll be glad to take care of any expense involved."

"He shouldn't be moved for several days, in my opinion," Doctor Aikerman replied. "He is in a state of semi-coma and will likely remain so for at least twenty-four hours."

"Who will stay with him?" Bess questioned in perplexity. "As far as we know, the man has no close friends or relatives."

"I'll remain here," Nancy offered quickly.

"That would mean you couldn't finish the golf tournament," said Mr. Drew. "And you have an excellent chance to win. I should prefer to hire a nurse."

"A man is really needed about the place," Nancy commented with a troubled frown. "Someone should take care of the animals."

"See here, why can't Bill and Bud and I stay?" Ned proposed suddenly. "We could look after everything. If the man should take a turn for the worse, we could call Doctor Aikerman right away."

"We'll be glad to do it," Bill Cowan added, whereupon Bud Mason nodded agreement.

"That would be a wonderful solution to the problem," Nancy said in relief, "but it doesn't seem fair to you boys. You came to Deer Mountain for a good time."

"That hotel is altogether too swanky for us," Ned declared with an indifferent shrug. "It would cost too much to stay there over the week-end. This place suits us."

After some discussion it was finally decided that the three boys would remain at the cabin.

In the event the patient should fail to improve within twenty-four hours, a trained nurse would be sent from the city. The physician gave the boys careful instructions as to how they were to care for the patient during his absence.

"I'll drop in again early tomorrow morning," he assured them. "Should there be any change before that time, notify me at once."

"Don't forget to take good care of the wild pets," Bess urged the boys.

"I wonder what one is supposed to feed a young mountain lion?" Ned asked in perplexity.

"We'll send out some raw meat when we get back to town," Mr. Drew promised, "as well as some bedding and a few things you may need here."

The Drew girl took Ned aside so that the others could not hear what she was saying.

"There's something I wish you'd do for me, Ned," she stated.

"Sure. What is it?"

"I want you to listen very carefully to anything that Mr. Haley—if that's who he is— may say while he's unconscious."

Ned glanced quickly at Nancy, but he refrained from asking for an explanation, even though he regarded the request as a strange one.

"I'll be glad to do it," he promised.

"I wish you'd take down every word in writing," Nancy added as she turned to leave the cabin. "The solution of a very perplexing mystery may depend upon your work."

CHAPTER XVI

An Unwanted Gift

"By the way, Dad, did you win your tennis match with Mr. Bartescue?" Nancy asked curiously as the car bumped along the road on its way back to the Deer Mountain Hotel.

"No, he defeated me two out of three sets," Mr. Drew admitted ruefully.

"Oh, I was almost certain you'd beat him, Dad. He must be a good player."

"Far better than I expected. We had a few close decisions as to whether balls were inside or outside the court, but I'm offering no alibis."

Nancy could easily imagine that Mortimer Bartescue would claim the benefit of any doubtful shot. She knew, too, that her father was too good a sport to argue with an opponent.

"A defeat now and then is good for anyone," Mr. Drew laughed lightly. "I don't believe in taking games too seriously."

At the hotel, after parting with the doctor, the lawyer explained to Nancy that it would be necessary for him to visit the nearby village to see about an important matter in connection with the jewel-theft case.

130

"May I go there with you?" Nancy inquired eagerly.

Mr. Drew smilingly shook his head. "I can't take you along this time, my dear. Anyway, you should be resting up for your match to-morrow."

After her father had driven away, Nancy and her chums inquired at the hotel desk to learn if any mail had arrived on the afternoon train. It was found that Bess and George had received letters from their parents, while for Nancy there was a note and a package. She studied the handwriting on them curiously.

"I'd say it is from Mortimer Bartescue!" George chuckled. "He's always trying to win your favor."

"Neither the envelope nor the package is addressed in his handwriting," Nancy replied, "that is, in any of his varied handwritings—for it always seems to be different."

"Hurry up and open the box," Bess advised impatiently. "I can't imagine what it contains."

At last Nancy had the wrapper removed. She held up a golf ball for her chums to see.

"Well, of all things to send a person, this takes the prize!"

The gift unquestionably had come from Mortimer Bartescue, for his name was auto-graphed neatly across the face of the golf ball.

"The note must explain about it," Bess de-clared. "Read it and see, Nancy."

The girl tore open the letter and found a two-line message from Mortimer Bartescue.

"I am sending you this ball to replace the one which you lost," he wrote. "Use it in the tournament tomorrow and win!"

"Well, of all the conceit!" Nancy Drew exclaimed indignantly. "I guess he thinks his autograph is just as important as Jimmy Harlow's."

"Will you play with the ball tomorrow?" Bess inquired mischievously.

"Certainly not! I'd like to send it back to him."

"That's what I'd do," George nodded. "Tell him you don't need any lucky ball to win the tournament!"

"No, I believe I'll keep this little souvenir after all," Nancy announced after a moment's thought. "It will serve as a specimen of Mr. Bartescue's handwriting. I'm interested in collecting as many of them as possible."

"Why does the man always use varied signatures?" Bess questioned in perplexity. "His handwriting never seems to be the same twice."

"I have a theory that he may be a forger," Nancy said in an undertone. "Perhaps my idea is a wild one, but how else can one explain it?"

"Why not report the man to the police?" George suggested promptly.

Nancy shook her head. "No, we can't do that. After all, a theory is not a proven fact

Besides, by playing a waiting game we may learn far more than we would if we were to expose the man immediately."

In a fanciful flight of imagination she could visualize Mortimer Bartescue linked with the international jewel-thief gang. The man's acquaintance with the mysterious Margaret Judson, as well as his manner of altering his signature, pointed to such a conclusion.

"Undoubtedly he came here to the Deer Mountain Hotel so that he might work with that woman!" Nancy told herself. "I'll never again have another thing to do with Mortimer Bartescue!"

However, a few minutes later as she was thinking over the matter in her room, the girl laughed at her own decision. After all, she had no evidence against Mortimer Bartescue. Even if he were a forger, that would be no reason for her avoiding him. On the contrary, if she considered herself anything of a detective she should make every effort to gain additional evidence to support her theory.

"By means of Mr. Bartescue I might be able to trace Margaret Judson," Nancy reflected soberly. "And I *must* find her."

Impulsively she sprang up from her chair. Slipping into her coat, she hastened downstairs. There was no time to tell her chums what she meant to do, for the bus for town would leave the hotel door in less than five minutes.

Nancy was the last passenger aboard, and as

the vehicle pulled away she wondered if she
were making a mistake to act without waiting
to consult her father. At the village she
alighted and entered a drug store. After making a purchase, she stepped into a telephone
booth.

She stood there debating for a moment, a
trifle fearful of what she was about to do.
Then, summoning her courage, she called the
Deer Mountain Hotel and asked to speak with
Mortimer Bartescue.

"It will be just my luck for him to be out,"
she thought anxiously.

A minute later she heard the man's voice at
the other end of the line.

"Hello, who is it?" he demanded impatiently
as Nancy, momentarily overcome by nervousness, remained silent.

"This—is—Miss Judson," Nancy stammered, trying to speak in a nasal tone.

"Your voice doesn't sound natural."

"I have a very bad cold. Can you hear m
now?"

"Yes, what is it that you wish, Miss Judson?
You know it isn't a good idea to call me here at
the hotel."

"I must speak with you about a very important matter. Can you meet me tonight?"

"Well, I had planned another engagement,"
Mr. Bartescue grumbled, "but I suppose I can.
Where shall we meet?"

"The same place as before."

"What's the matter with 2 B X Gardenia?" the man asked.

Nancy was nonplussed at such a reply, and for a moment could think of nothing to say. She had not the slightest idea as to the meaning of 2 B X Gardenia. In sheer desperation she mumbled into the telephone:

"Nothing but the weather," and hung up the receiver before Mr. Bartescue could make any response.

As Nancy walked to the bus stop, she felt thoroughly irritated at the outcome of the telephone conversation. Had she betrayed herself to Mortimer Bartescue?

"What can be the meaning of 2 B X Gardenia?" she speculated. "It must be a code word to designate a meeting place."

The telephone conversation had served one purpose at least—to convince Nancy that Margaret Judson and Mortimer Bartescue were working together in some nefarious business which would not bear the light of honest investigation.

"I must learn more," she told herself, "and the only way is to follow Mortimer Bartescue tonight and find out where he goes."

Returning to the hotel, Nancy explained her plan to Bess and George. Her intention was to borrow Ned Nickerson's car and use it to follow Mr. Bartescue when he should go to keep his appointment with Margaret Judson.

The car was parked near the hotel exit, to be

ready at a moment's notice. The girls then went to dinner as usual, and were pleased to observe that Mortimer Bartescue had entered the dining room ahead of them.

Before the girls were even half through dinner Mr. Bartescue abruptly arose and left the dining room.

"We'll not take dessert tonight," Nancy said hurriedly to the waiter.

The chums reached the lobby in time to see the man depart by the front door. They saw him glance anxiously at his wrist watch as he stepped into his automobile.

"He intends to keep an appointment, all right," Nancy declared in satisfaction. "Come on, girls, we must move fast or he'll be out of sight!"

They ran to their own parked car and had it started in a twinkling. The other automobile had vanished down the road, but Nancy drove rapidly and soon came within view of it again.

"He seems to be heading for the village," she observed aloud. "Don't take your eyes from that taillight."

Apparently unaware that he was being followed, Bartescue drove into town, parking his auto across the street from a moving picture theatre. Nancy halted nearly a half block away lest she be observed. The girls saw the man look at his watch again, then cross the street and enter the amusement place.

"Do you suppose he expects to meet Miss

Judson inside the building?" Bess asked in disappointment. "Perhaps he's just attending a show."

"Wait here and I'll find out," Nancy said, sliding from behind the steering wheel.

She bought an admission ticket to the theatre and went inside.

"A tall dark man just entered a moment ago," she said to the usher. "Can you show me where he is seated?"

"You must be mistaken," the usher replied politely. "The last persons were two girls, and before them an elderly couple."

Nancy knew that Mortimer Bartescue had entered the theatre, even though the usher could not recall him by her description. In the darkened room she was unable to distinguish faces.

Thinking that possibly the man might have gone to the lounge to keep his appointment with Margaret Judson, she went there. The room was empty.

In perplexity Nancy returned to the lobby, and after standing there for several minutes she finally decided to join her chums again. She left the theatre and crossed the street.

Suddenly she halted in astonishment, staring blankly at the place where she had parked Ned's car. Bess, George and the automobile had vanished.

CHAPTER XVII

The Missing Car

Nancy was dismayed for an instant, fearing that during her absence harm had befallen her chums. However, a little sober reflection convinced her that George and Bess must have driven off somewhere deliberately.

"Very likely Mortimer Bartescue came out of the theatre shortly after I went inside," she reasoned. "The girls may have decided to trail him."

Nancy's position was an awkward one, for without a car she was temporarily stranded in the village. A bus would not make the run back to the Deer Mountain Hotel for nearly an hour.

Since there seemed to be nothing else for her to do, Nancy entered a nearby drug store. Seating herself by a window, she ordered an ice cream soda. She hoped that by the time she should have finished it, Bess and George would have returned.

Half an hour elapsed, and still there was no sign of the missing car. Nancy glanced anxiously at her watch. The bus would soon be due and she must decide whether to return to the hotel or continue her vigil.

"George and Bess may not come back for hours," she told herself. "I believe I'd better return to the hotel."

Nancy paid for the soda and stepped out on the street again. As she made her way toward the bus stop she heard the screech of brakes. Then a car came to a sudden halt by the curb.

"Nancy!" called a voice.

She whirled about to see Ned Nickerson, who had driven up. He was driving his own machine.

"Why Ned, how did you get here?"

The boy sprang out to open the car door for her.

"Bess and George sent me after you," he explained. "They're back at the hotel."

"At the hotel? Well, I like the way they deserted me!"

"They didn't mean to run off, but right after you left Mortimer Bartescue came out of the theatre by a side door. The girls knew you were eager to trail him, so they followed in the car."

"Where did he go?" Nancy inquired feverishly.

"He merely drove back to the hotel. I happened to be there when the girls arrived, for I wanted to talk to you. They asked me to come back after you."

"Oh, I'm disappointed at the way Mortimer

Bartescue gave us the slip,'' Nancy said impatiently. ''I wonder if he didn't suspect he was being followed after all?''

Suddenly recalling that Ned had said he wished to talk to her, she anxiously inquired if the old man at the cabin had taken a turn for the worse.

''He seems about the same, Nancy, but he has been talking a great deal. He revealed his name as Joe Haley.''

''And did you take down his words, Ned?''

''Yes. His mutterings were so strange that I thought you'd want to hear them right away. I have everything he said written down on a paper. His most startling words were these:

'' 'Miss Margaret, I'm afraid the box was stolen—don't cry, Miss Margaret—why don't you marry Morton?' ''

''Are you sure the name was Morton?'' Nancy asked quickly. ''It couldn't have been Mortimer?''

''It might have been. I admit I didn't hear what he said very clearly.''

''Ned, I forgot to ask you about Mr. Bartescue. Did you look to see if his name appears in the Social Register?''

''I looked for it but it wasn't there. I imagine the fellow is just a windbag.''

''I've suspected it all along, Ned, but his connection with Margaret Judson amazes me. There are some angles to the case which I can't fathom.''

During the ride back to the hotel, Nancy told the young man as much as she could about the affair which had brought her father to the Deer Mountain Hotel. Some of the facts in her possession were confidential. Without Mr. Drew's permission, she would not divulge them.

"When you return to Mr. Haley's cabin listen closely to anything he may say regarding Margaret Judson," she urged.

"I will," Ned promised, "and if I learn anything worth while I'll report to you at once."

During Nancy's absence from the hotel Carson Drew had returned from a fruitless journey to Hemlock Hall.

"I acted upon a tip," he explained to Nancy as they talked together in his room late that night. "It was a worthless one, as usual."

"You seem tired and discouraged this evening, Dad."

"Oh, I'm a little fed up with this case. To tell you the truth, I half suspect we've been on the wrong track from the first."

"How do you mean?"

"I doubt that Margaret Judson has anything to do with the affair. There's no real evidence to support our theory that the brass chest belonged to her. I'm inclined to get back to my legal work on this particular case and let the New York detectives solve their own problem as to how to locate the guilty persons. After all, that's not my business—I was merely trying to help out."

"I rather enjoyed doing the detective work," Nancy said regretfully.

"There's no reason why you can't go on with it. I simply haven't the time myself."

"I don't suppose I can glean many clues after we're back at River Heights," Nancy said ruefully.

"Oh, we'll not be leaving here for a few days. You still have plenty of time, both for your detective work and the golf tournament."

"Speaking of golf, I guess I should be getting to bed," Nancy declared with a gay laugh. "Tomorrow I face the crucial test and I must be rested."

"How does your hand feel?" her father inquired anxiously. "Did you see the doctor?"

"Yes, he let me take off the bandage, but said I must be very careful or the old pain would come back."

"It's a shame you must play with such a handicap," Mr. Drew said sympathetically. "I'm banking on you to win, anyway!"

"Thanks, Dad," Nancy smiled as she turned away. "I'll do my best, you may be sure of that."

She dropped in for a moment at her chums' room. George was writing letters, while Bess, propped up with pillows, had been reading in bed.

"Is your story a good one?" Nancy inquired with interest.

"It's supposed to be a serious book and I

can't make head nor tail of it," Bess complained. "Here, take a look at the crazy thing."

She gave the book a careless toss, expecting that her chum would catch it. Nancy had been looking in another direction, and before she could make a move the heavy volume had struck her injured hand.

"Oh!" she exclaimed, trying to smother a cry of pain.

Bess leaped from bed and ran to her chum's side.

"Oh, Nancy, I didn't mean to do it," she wailed. "Your poor finger! I thought you were watching when I tossed the book."

"Don't blame yourself," Nancy said, trying to smile. "It will stop hurting in a minute."

"I'll never forgive myself," Bess said contritely. "I don't know what possessed me to do such a thing."

"The finger feels better already," Nancy assured her chum kindly. "Please don't worry about it, Bess."

"But your match tomorrow——"

"The pain will go away before then, I'm sure. Jump back into bed, Bess, and forget it."

Somewhat reassured, Bess did as she was bidden. She had no idea that Nancy actually suffered far more intense pain than she would admit.

A little later, in her own room, Nancy prepared for bed, but she was unable to sleep.

The ache in her hand steadily grew worse until she paced the floor from sheer nervousness.

"This will never do," she told herself sternly. "I must get some sleep or I'll never be able to play tomorrow."

The hour was still early, so Nancy decided to dress and seek the house physician. Without troubling either her father or her chums she went to Doctor Aikerman's office.

"What have you been doing to this hand?" he inquired sternly.

Nancy explained about the accident, and was dismayed when the man shook his head sadly as if to indicate that there was little he could do for her.

"I hope you are not planning to play in the golf tournament tomorrow, Miss Drew."

"Oh, but I am, Doctor! Please, you'll not refuse me permission?"

"That is a matter for you to decide, Miss Drew. Your injury will not prove a permanent one, but I should judge that you suffer excruciating pain."

"I do," Nancy admitted ruefully. "I was hoping you could help relieve it."

"There is very little I can do except put on another bandage. It will require time to heal."

"The pain is so acute I haven't been able to sleep."

"I can give you something for that," the doctor said. "A mild sleeping potion will help you rest during the night, and perhaps by morning the pain will have lessened considerably."

Nancy thanked the doctor, and when she was back in her room again she took the medicine as directed. Soon she dropped into sleep, and did not awaken until the sun streamed into the window the following morning. As she opened her eyes she heard some one rapping on a door.

"May George and I come in?" Bess called.

"Not dressed yet?" George asked in surprise. Then, as she noticed how tired and wan her chum appeared, she added quickly, "Nancy, you've had a bad night!"

"I slept fairly well after the doctor gave me some medicine."

"The doctor!" Bess exclaimed in dismay. "Oh, Nancy, you didn't let on that your hand hurt you very much. Why did I have to do a dreadful thing like that?"

"Now don't start worrying," Nancy said firmly. "It hurts only a little this morning, and I intend to play in the golf tournament anyway."

"But you'll be badly handicapped," Bess wailed. "It isn't fair at all."

Nancy refused to say anything more about her injury, and started to dress. George and Bess put on her shoes for her and tried in every way to assist her so that she would not need to use her sore hand.

"You'll have just time enough to eat breakfast and reach the first tee," George advised, glancing at her watch. "It's rather late."

The girls hastened down to the dining room. Scarcely had they seated themselves when Nancy glimpsed Sammy Sutter coming timidly toward her.

"Excuse me for bothering you, Miss Drew, but I want to talk to you about something important."

"Today's match?" Nancy questioned with a smile, looking up from the menu card.

The boy shook his head. "No, it's about Miss Judson. My mother is here in the lobby and she has something to tell you about the woman."

Nancy arose abruptly, her eyes alight with anticipation.

"Don't wait breakfast for me," she told Bess and George. "I'll go with Sammy, for this may be important!"

CHAPTER XVIII

Caught by the Storm

"What have you learned about Miss Margaret Judson?" Nancy inquired eagerly as she led Mrs. Samuel Sutter Sr. to a secluded nook in the hotel lobby. "Do you know where she is living now?"

"No, Miss Drew," the woman admitted, "that's what I want to talk with you about."

The girl looked puzzled, and Mrs. Sutter hastened to explain her purpose in coming to the hotel. She had learned from the village postmistress that several letters which were in the same handwriting, and all addressed to Margaret Judson, were being held for lack of a forwarding address.

"I thought you might have found out where the woman lives, Miss Drew."

"Oh, no," Nancy answered, trying not to disclose her annoyance, "I am as much in the dark as ever."

It was clear to her now that Mrs. Sutter had come, not to impart information, but to learn if she possibly could why Nancy was interested in Margaret Judson. She cleverly avoided the woman's questions, but could not help feeling provoked because so much time had been wasted.

"I really know almost nothing about Margaret Judson," she told Mrs. Sutter. "I am not even familiar with the name of the professor to whom she was engaged."

"I heard it once, but I can't recall it now," Mrs. Sutter said regretfully. She seemed in a mood to prolong the conversation, but Nancy cut her short by explaining that her chums were waiting for her at the breakfast table.

Bess and George had just finished their meal. Since it was now so late, Nancy ordered nothing more than breakfast rolls.

"You can't win a golf tournament on a diet like that," Bess protested.

"There's no time for more. I wasted twenty minutes with Mrs. Sutter and learned practically nothing! The woman is a gossip, I fear, and merely wished to gather information about Miss Judson so she could spread it about."

The girls hastened to the golf office, there to find the tournament chairman talking earnestly with a group of men and women players who were to compete in the day's finals.

"The matches have been postponed until one o'clock," Nancy's opponent, Miss Howard, explained. "There seems to be some mix-up."

"That is entirely satisfactory to me," Nancy declared in relief. "I really should prefer to play this afternoon."

Bess and George suggested to their chum that she retire to her hotel room for a rest, but the girl had other plans. Taking her father's car, she drove first to the village, there to interview the postmistress. The woman was very glad to show Nancy the letters which she was holding for Margaret Judson.

"I believe Mortimer Bartescue wrote them all," the girl thought as she studied the handwriting. "At least, many of the characters resemble those which appear on my autographed ball. Now I wonder——"

Nancy's second point of call was at the nearby college town of Andover. Selecting a bookstore directly across from the campus, she asked for a college register and was permitted to look at the latest record of students and instructors.

Nancy ran rapidly through the list of professors, searching for one whose first name might be Morton. She felt highly elated when she came upon an instructor of philosophy named Morton Teusch. Her confident feeling that she had located Miss Judson's former fiance vanished, when in searching through the rest of the list she discovered two other Mortons, a Professor Hilburn and a man by the name of Wardell.

"I guess I shall have to call on all three," Nancy thought wearily. "I'll have to hurry too, or I'll not get back to the Deer Mountain Hotel in time for my golf match."

Morton Teusch was not difficult to locate.

His office was listed as Room 305 of the Liberal Arts Building. Nancy found the professor to be an elderly, white-haired gentleman of nearly seventy years of age. Since he could not by any stretch of the imagination be connected with so youthful a person as Margaret Judson, Nancy retreated without even revealing to him the purpose of her call.

Professor Hilburn was not in his office. The girl spent many precious minutes trying to find his home in the residential section. Even before she rapped on the door of the neat little brick house she suspected that she had made another mistake, for an upset kiddie cart on the front porch gave mute evidence that the person she had come to see was not a single man. Mrs. Hilburn proved to be a charming, middle-aged woman with three children, and she assured Nancy that she had been married for nearly fifteen years.

"I shouldn't have troubled you," the girl apologized. "The professor for whom I am searching is single, and I know only his first name, which is Morton."

"I wonder if you could mean Professor Morton Wardell?" the woman inquired thoughtfully. "He is a single man, and not more than thirty years old, I should judge. He is the head of our zoology and botany departments."

"I believe he must be the man for whom I am looking," Nancy said eagerly. "Can you tell me how to reach his home?"

"He has none of his own, but rooms on Melburn street."

Ten minutes later found Nancy ringing the doorbell of a large colonial house. She was admitted by a pleasant, white-haired woman.

"Professor Wardell isn't here just now," the landlady replied in response to Nancy's inquiry. "Sometimes he comes home for lunch, but I never can be certain."

"I stopped at his office but he was not in."

"No, I doubt that he would be there today. He usually takes a hike somewhere into the woods. Professor Wardell is deeply interested in nature lore."

Nancy was disappointed that she could not see the man, especially since she was inclined to believe that he might be the person she was seeking. Deciding to take the landlady into her confidence a little, she mentioned that she was trying to locate a man who was an acquaintance of Margaret Judson.

"Oh, dear me, they were more than mere acquaintances," the woman replied quickly. "I am certain Professor Wardell and Miss Judson were engaged. But the marriage failed to take place. He hasn't seemed himself since. He is quiet and subdued. It makes my heart fairly ache to see him so sad, for I have never known a finer man."

Nancy was now convinced that Morton Wardell was the person with whom she must talk if she expected to solve the mystery which surrounded Margaret Judson's strange actions. She dared not tarry longer in Andover lest she be late for her golf match.

"I should like to have you give Professor Wardell an important message," the girl requested the woman.

"Yes, certainly."

Nancy took a calling card from her purse. After writing the name of her hotel on it, she gave it to the woman.

"Please ask Professor Wardell to see me at this address just as soon as he can. Tell him that I should like to talk with him about a most important matter."

"I'll give him your message," the woman promised. "Professor Wardell is very obliging, so I feel certain he'll come to the hotel either tonight or tomorrow."

While on her way back to the village and then on to the Deer Mountain Hotel, Nancy reflected that her morning had been far from wasted. She thought it rather significant that both Professor Wardell and old Mr. Haley were interested in botany and zoology.

"I wonder if there might not be a connection between the two men," she thought idly.

Arriving at the hotel, Nancy barely had time to snatch a sandwich before she was due to appear at the first tee. Bess, George, Ned and Mr. Drew were on hand to witness the start of the match, and smiled encouragingly as the girl stood quietly waiting her turn to drive off.

"Bring home the silver loving cup!" George urged in a whisper. "We'll be pulling for you every bit of the way."

"How does your hand feel?" Bess asked anxiously.

"Pretty good," Nancy replied carelessly, for she knew that her chum still felt guilty about the accident of the previous evening. "The thing that worries me is the skill of my opponent. I'm afraid she'll defeat me."

Miss Howard, a golfer well known throughout the state, had turned in a score of eighty-nine for her semi-final match, which was a better one than Nancy had ever made. The Drew girl knew that if she expected to win the finals she would have to shoot the best game of her life. She feared that with her hand paining her as it did, she might be unable to play even as well as usual.

"I'll just do the best I can. Win or lose, I'll try to accept my fate gracefully," she told herself.

Miss Howard made a long drive from the tee. Nancy's ball did not go as far, but ended up in perfect position. Both putted well when they reached the green, and the score was even.

The second and the third holes likewise were tied, making it evident to Nancy that the match promised to be a close one. At the fourth hole she gained the advantage when Miss Howard's ball lodged in a bunker, but the fifth hole found them even again. On through the sixth and seventh they played, fighting grimly for the lead.

So absorbed were both girls in their game that they scarcely noticed how overcast the sky had become. Black clouds rolled swiftly up from the west, blotting out the sun.

The ninth hole, marking the halfway point of the match, left the girls still even. Miss Howard seemed as fresh as ever, and on the tenth tee drove out a ball which easily went two hundred and twenty yards.

"A beautiful drive," Nancy praised as she stepped forward to take her turn.

She swung with all her strength, connecting squarely with the ball, but at the same instant a severe pain shot through her injured hand. Nancy suffered intensely, and it was all she could do to grip the club. As a result her next shot was a dismal failure.

Quick to seize an advantage, Miss Howard, playing beautiful golf, took the hole easily. The eleventh likewise fell to her, and Nancy, two down, began to fear that the match was lost.

"I can't give up," she told herself grimly. "I must ignore the pain and swing into each shot with all my strength."

As the girls teed off at the twelfth hole, a few drops of rain spattered against their faces. Miss Howard glanced anxiously at the sky.

"It looks like a hard rain coming up," she declared nervously. "I am afraid of storms."

By the time the two reached the twelfth green it was raining steadily. In trying to hurry, Miss Howard missed her putt and the hole went to Nancy, leaving her now only one down. She must make up that point!

The thirteenth and fourteenth, played in a drenching rain, were halved, leaving the score the same as before. By this time the wind had sprung up. As the girls made their way to the fifteenth tee it was all they could do to maintain their balance.

"This is terrible!" Miss Howard exclaimed. "Surely the committee can't expect us to finish our match in this kind of weather."

"It is getting worse every minute, too," Nancy stated, drawing her thin sweater closer about her. "The main part of the storm hasn't even struck yet."

Miss Howard hesitated a moment, then abruptly handed her driver to the caddy.

"I'm going back to the hotel," she announced. "If the committee says we may continue the match tomorrow, all well and good. If not, then I'll default."

"No, we'll stop play by mutual agreement," Nancy replied. "I fell certain no one would blame us for failing to finish under these conditions."

The rain began to fall in torrents. Miss Howard, followed by the two caddies, ran as fast as she could toward the hotel. Nancy darted into the woods, and there, partly pro-

tected by the trees, made up her mind that the
Haley cabin was closer than any other shelter.

The wind was steadily rising, and as she ran
through the woods, the tree boughs crashed
together overhead. The air was filled with flying leaves, while now and then a dead limb
came plunging downward.

Approaching the haunted bridge, Nancy was
startled to hear the same moaning sound which
had been heard on a previous visit to the
locality.

"It must be the wind howling through the
ravine," she told herself. "But regardless of
what it is, I'll not turn back."

Nancy reached the sagging bridge where the
old scarecrow, wet and tattered, was dancing
wildly in the wind. It seemed more ghost-like
than ever, and as the girl hurried past, the
spindly "arms" entwined themselves about
her body. She shook herself free, and by a
supreme effort pushed on.

The bridge swayed in the wind. As Nancy
reached mid-stream it suddenly creaked and
groaned. The underpinning had been torn
away!

As the structure swung around, Nancy
clutched the railing for support, but it too was
unsound. The decayed wood gave way, and the
girl plunged violently forward to meet the
turbulent waters of the swollen stream.

CHAPTER XIX

An Unexpected Visitor

THE current was swift, and before Nancy could battle her way to shore she found herself carried far below the point where the haunted bridge had stood. Bedraggled, and with her clothes muddy and torn, she pulled herself out onto the slippery bank and sat there for a moment in the rain, trying to regain her breath.

"Bess warned me I'd get into trouble if I insisted upon coming here," she told herself ruefully, "and I guess she was right. The old haunted bridge won the last laugh."

With her clothes thoroughly soaked and her hair plastered against her face, Nancy was anything but presentable. She scarcely knew whether or not to continue on to the Haley cabin.

"I'll never dare enter the hotel looking this way," she thought. "I'll have to go somewhere and dry myself first."

Nancy scrambled up the bank and followed the ravine trail to the cabin. Her firm knock brought Ned to the door.

"Why Nancy, what has happened?" he cried

151

in astonishment. "I thought you were playing your golf match——"

"I was," the girl laughed as she stepped into the kitchen, "but I decided to drop in for a moment and borrow an umbrella. Did you hear a loud crash a few minutes ago?"

"Yes, we thought it sounded as if the bridge went down."

"It did. And I went with it. You should have seen me swimming down the ravine!" Abandoning her bantering tone, Nancy added quickly, "I'm surprised to find you here, Ned, for I understood you intended to stay at the hotel until the end of the golf match."

"I meant to, Nancy, but just after you teed off Bill came to tell me I was needed here again."

"Mr. Haley is worse?"

"He's been restless, and the boys don't like to be in the house alone with him. Bill and Bud are outside now trying to look after the animals. I should be helping them."

"I'll stay here with Mr. Haley," Nancy offered quickly. "You look after the animals."

Before Ned could protest she had moved quietly to the adjoining bedroom to peer at the patient. At the moment the man was resting peacefully, and judging from the appearance of his face his condition remained unchanged.

After Ned had donned a raincoat and left the cabin, Nancy tiptoed to a closet in search of warm garments. The only clothes available were a pair of slacks and an old blue shirt, a costume which gave her the appearance of a handsome boy.

While she was hanging her own wet clothes by the stove to dry she heard Mr. Haley stir restlessly, and hastened back to his bedside. The old man's eyes were wide open. His gaze wandered slowly about the room and came to rest upon Nancy's face.

"Who are you?" he asked in a whisper. "What are you doing here?"

"I am Nancy Drew, and I have come to help you."

The old man shook his head in a baffled manner.

"Nancy is a girl's name," he mumbled. "You are a boy. The house is filled with boys. Why are they here in my cabin?"

Nancy tried to explain the situation to him but Mr. Haley did not wish to listen. He raised himself on an elbow, motioning her to assist him from his bed.

"No, you must remain quiet," Nancy told him firmly. "You must not get up until the doctor says you may."

"But I have to! My animals will starve. How long have I been ill?"

"Now don't get excited," Nancy said soothingly. "Everything is all right. Your animals are being well fed and cared for by friends. Just lie back on your pillow and try to get some rest."

Her words reassured Mr. Haley, and he obediently remained quiet for several minutes. However, his eyes kept roving to her face, and she knew he was trying to rationalize the situation.

Nancy was eager to ask the old man some questions, but she knew she should do nothing which would excite him. Until the doctor should determine that he was past danger of a relapse she must not even mention Margaret Judson's name to him.

Presently Mr. Haley fell into a peaceful sleep. By the time Ned and his chums came in out of the storm, Nancy was able to report that she considered the patient well on the road to recovery.

"That's good news," Ned said in obvious relief. "To tell you the truth, Bud and Bill and I have been pretty closely confined here. We'd like to have a chance to see the sights of Deer Mountain before our vacation is over."

"It was good of you boys to help us out the way you did."

"Oh, we wanted to do it," Ned said hastily, fearing that Nancy might misunderstand.

As the storm subsided, the boys listened eagerly to an account of the day's golf match. They were disappointed that play had ended on the fifteenth hole with Nancy one down, but they were confident she would defeat her opponent when the match should be resumed.

After the rain ceased, Ned and his friends

set off for the ravine to view the fallen bridge.
They found that it had floated some distance
down stream and was lodged against an old log.
Returning to the cabin for ropes and tools, they
set about the task of pulling the structure back
into place and anchoring it securely.

During the absence of the boys Nancy donned
her own clothes. Then, thoroughly worn out
from her strenuous day, she sat down in a
chair by Mr. Haley's bedside and fell asleep.
She was aroused by hearing a knock on the
door.

"I wonder who it can be?" she asked herself
as she arose to answer the summons. "Ned
or the boys wouldn't bother to rap."

She opened the door to face a tall, handsome
man who appeared to be about thirty years of
age. Evidently he had not expected to see a
girl at the cabin, for he stared at Nancy and
then quickly lowered his eyes as if aware that
he was being rude.

"I beg your pardon," he said politely. "Is
Mr. Haley at home?"

"Yes, but I'm not sure that he can see a
visitor," Nancy responded. "He was injured
in an accident and is confined to his bed."

"Oh, are you a nurse?" the man questioned
in alarm. "I had no idea anything was wrong
here or I'd have come before this. Mr. Haley
isn't in grave danger, is he?"

"He is recovering now."

"That's good," the man said in relief. "Do

you think I might see him for a few minutes?
My name is Wardell and Mr. Haley is my
uncle.''

Nancy was taken completely by surprise.
Recovering quickly, she invited the young man
to enter the cabin.

''Mr. Haley is sleeping now,'' she explained,
''but when he awakens you may be able to
speak with him for a moment.''

''I'd rather not do it if you feel it would
excite him,'' Mr. Wardell said anxiously. ''I
think the world of my uncle. He practically
reared me, and it was through him that I became interested in nature lore. I've always felt
that I might never have entered my chosen field
if it hadn't been for Mr. Haley.''

Nancy asked a few polite questions concerning the man's work. Although now she was
perfectly aware that he was a professor at
Andover College, she preferred not to reveal
her knowledge to him.

''I came over to the Deer Mountain Hotel
this afternoon to see a young woman who requested me to call upon an important matter,''
the caller explained. ''Apparently it could not
have been very important for she wasn't even
waiting for me. Since I was so near by I
thought I'd drop over and see my uncle, never
dreaming that he had been injured. Can you
tell me about the accident?''

Nancy supplied details, and then switched the
subject back to Professor Wardell's work at the

college. She wished to bring Margaret Judson's name into the conversation, yet she scarcely knew how to do so without appearing abrupt.

"When Mr. Haley first was injured we were afraid he had no living relatives," she remarked, watching the young man closely. "However, I did find a picture of a beautiful girl here in the cabin but there was no way positively to establish her identity."

She found the photograph of Margaret Judson and placed it in Professor Wardell's hands. The young man stared at it without speaking. The expression of deep anguish upon his face made Nancy feel almost sorry that she had shown it to him.

"From Mr. Haley's remarks when he was semi-conscious I gathered that he knew this girl well," she said casually. "Seemingly she lived near here and fled when her home burned."

"Yes, that is true." The professor kept his gaze averted.

"Perhaps you recognize the picture?"

"Could I ever forget it?" the young man asked, his voice husky with emotion. "Margaret Judson and I were engaged to be married."

"Oh, I'm sorry——"

"You couldn't have known," the man said quickly, little suspecting that Nancy deliberately had opened the old wound. "I was away on a scientific expedition at the time Margaret's house was destroyed by fire. Everything was lost.''

"Everything?" Nancy inquired in disappointment.

"Well, she did save a box of jewelry." Professor Wardell smiled grimly. "Among other things it contained the engagement ring I had given her."

"How fortunate," Nancy murmured.

"It was anything but fortunate. In her flight Margaret lost the box. She left a note for me, saying that while she loved me dearly she must break our engagement. I couldn't understand her actions then and I cannot now. Why should she refuse to marry me just because the ring was lost? I'd be only too happy to buy Margaret a dozen rings."

"Perhaps she was afraid you would be angry."

"The ring was a valuable one, I admit, but I'm sure Margaret knew me well enough to realize that I'd not blame her for something which obviously couldn't have been her fault. I've tried to locate her, but after the fire she disappeared. I'd give anything to find her again."

Nancy was tempted to tell the young man that she believed Miss Judson to be somewhere in the vicinity of Deer Mountain, but she wisely decided not to build up any false hopes in his mind. She felt fairly certain the carved chest which had come into her possession was the lost property of the young woman, and she rather suspected too that she knew the reason why Margaret Judson had broken her engagement.

Nancy liked Professor Wardell very much and was eager to help him. However, she thought that her father should be the one to decide how much information should be revealed to him.

"After you have visited your uncle for a few minutes I'd like to have you come with me to the Deer Mountain Hotel," Nancy told the man cordially. "I am very eager to have you meet my father."

"I'll be delighted to talk with him," Professor Wardell said politely, "especially since I'd like to thank him for being so kind to my uncle. However, I must confess I don't know his name —or yours either, for that matter."

Nancy enjoyed the young man's look of astonishment as she replied with a smile:

"I happen to be the girl who asked you to call at the Deer Mountain Hotel. My name is Nancy Drew."

CHAPTER XX

GATHERING EVIDENCE

"You are Nancy Drew?" Professor Wardell stammered, taken back by the girl's revelation of her identity. "Why did you send for me? Have you learned anything about Margaret Judson?"

"I have found something which I think may belong to her," Nancy replied.

"Not the box of jewelry?"

"I can't tell you now. You must talk with my father first."

The professor did not press Nancy further for an explanation. However, after they had conversed for a few minutes he did ask her permission to enter Mr. Haley's bedroom. His uncle was still asleep, so after standing by the bedside for a short time, the man quietly returned to the kitchen.

Presently Ned, Bud and Bill trudged wearily in, spent by their attempt to repair the bridge. They reported to Nancy that while they had it in fairly good condition, considerable work yet remained to be done on it and the structure was not very safe.

"You'll not be able to cross the ravine in returning to your hotel," Ned told her. "I'll drive you back in my car."

"Thank you, Ned, but that won't be necessary. Professor Wardell has promised to take me in his automobile which is parked up by the old Judson estate."

The boys had failed to observe the stranger, for he had been sitting quietly in a dark corner of the room. They were therefore somewhat embarrassed as they responded to an introduction. Ned could not help but glance at the man a trifle jealously, wondering at his apparent friendship with Nancy. Even the information that the man was Mr. Haley's nephew did not satisfy him entirely. He felt that she displayed a decided eagerness to have the professor escort her back to the hotel in his stead.

Nancy gladly would have revealed the facts in the case to Ned, but with Bud and Bill hovering so near, an explanation was out of the question. In leaving the cabin she gave the boy a warm smile and bade him take good care of the patient.

"I don't seem to be of much use at anything else," Ned muttered, turning away.

During the drive back to the Deer Mountain Hotel, Nancy was troubled by her friend's attitude, but she soon dismissed the matter from her mind. She knew that she would be able to take Ned into her confidence before another day should elapse.

Leaving Professor Wardell in the hotel lobby, she sought her father, who was in his room.

"Dad!" she cried, bursting in upon him. "I'm almost certain that the carved chest which I found in the ravine is Miss Judson's missing property! I have just met Professor Wardell, the young woman's former fiancé, and I want you to talk to him. If you feel that he can be trusted, let's take him into our confidence."

"I'd very much like to meet this young man," Carson Drew replied after he had heard his daughter's story. "Bring him here to my room where we can talk things over privately."

Nancy was not disappointed at the outcome of the interview, for the two men took an immediate liking to each other. She was secretly elated when her father broached the topic of his search for Miss Judson.

"I appreciate your opinion, sir," Professor Wardell said respectfully after he had listened to a summary of the evidence against the young woman, "but I cannot believe that Miss Judson knows anything about the missing jewels. She was always such an honorable person and comes from a fine family. I cannot conceive that she can have any connection with an international gang of thieves."

"That's my opinion exactly," Nancy declared, nodding vigorously.

"Nevertheless, there are a few clues which seem to connect her with the affair," Mr. Drew

commented, hoping to gain additional information from the professor. "For instance, a
jeweled vanity case. Do you know if Miss
Judson had one?"

"Not to my knowledge, although she was
very fond of jewelry. To tell you the truth, I
never noticed particularly."

"Another question: Have you ever heard
Miss Judson speak of a man by the name of
Mortimer Bartescue?"

"Why yes, I seem to recall that he was an
acquaintance of hers. I believe she met him in
Europe."

Nancy and her father exchanged quick
glances. Here was information which tended
to link the young woman with the jewel smuggling case. Of course, it had not been proved
that Mortimer Bartescue was a crook, but the
various methods he used to alter his handwriting tended to suggest strongly that he was a
fugitive from justice.

"Is Mortimer Bartescue under suspicion?"
Professor Wardell questioned anxiously.

"Yes," Carson Drew answered gravely, "but
so far the evidence against him is purely cir-
cumstantial. If only we could find Miss Judson,
she might be able to clear up the mystery surrounding both of them."

"I have no idea where Miss Judson can be
now," the professor replied thoughtfully.
"She might be staying with a cousin at Rock
City."

"You have never investigated the lead yourself?" Nancy inquired in surprise.

"No," the man answered in a low tone. "You see, I didn't want to force my attentions upon Miss Judson. However, I still believe that if I could talk with her everything might be explained and cleared up. I don't feel that I should seek her out deliberately without some indication from her that she would like to see me again."

"I understand how you feel," Nancy said sympathetically.

The hour was growing late. Professor Wardell arose to leave, for he was already late for an important meeting.

"I should like to keep in touch with you," Carson Drew said as he escorted the young man to the door.

"Yes indeed, I'll be waiting eagerly to hear from you again, Mr. Drew. Your daughter has my address at Andover. When I am not there I usually can be reached at my office in the science hall. If you receive any news of Miss Judson I shall appreciate deeply being notified."

After the professor had gone, Nancy and her father discussed the case for a few minutes but were unable to reach any conclusion as to the innocence or guilt of Mortimer Bartescue. His association with Margaret Judson actually proved nothing, for as yet they had established no case against the young woman.

"In spite of all the evidence against her, I can't help but believe, as does Professor Wardell, that she had nothing to do with the jewel theft," Nancy declared confidently. "That was also your opinion at first, Dad."

"Quite true," the lawyer nodded. "I admit this case has me baffled, for never before have I encountered one with so many contradictory features."

Presently Mr. Drew and his daughter gave up trying to figure out the puzzle, turning their attention to another pressing matter. During her brief stay at Mr. Haley's cabin Nancy had observed that many articles were needed to make the patient more comfortable. She suggested to her father that they drive out before dinner, taking with them the necessary supplies. The car was loaded with groceries as well as other articles, including a few good books which Nancy thought Ned and his chums might enjoy reading.

"I'm afraid they've been having a pretty dull time of it since coming to Deer Mountain," she told her father regretfully. "This afternoon when I talked with Ned he seemed especially blue."

"The boys deserve a little outing," Mr. Drew replied. "We'll see—perhaps I can help with that a bit."

Ned was alone with the patient when Nancy and her father reached the cabin. He explained that Bud and Bill were down at the ravine working on the foot bridge. A short time later the boys came trudging in, tired and hungry, but pleased to report that they had finished the repairs.

Nancy set about preparing a warm meal. Later the boys declared that it was the first really good cooking they had tasted since they had left River Heights.

"How would you fellows like to have the evening off?" Carson drew inquired after the dishes had been cleared away. "I'll be glad to stay here with Mr. Haley if you think you would like a little fun."

"Say, that would be great!" Ned exclaimed. "Is there a dance at the hotel tonight, Nancy?"

"Yes, there is. I imagine Bess and George would like to attend it, too."

"Then we'll make it a party!" Ned declared enthusiastically. "Come on, fellows, let's change into our dancing duds!"

While the boys were making themselves presentable for the party, Nancy and her father sat with old Mr. Haley in the adjoining room.

"How are you feeling?" Mr. Drew questioned gently as he observed that the patient's eyes were open.

"Better," the old man responded in a low voice. "Only weak."

"That is to be expected," Nancy said soothingly. "You have been very ill."

She did not wish to excite Mr. Haley by saying any more, but he seemed to want her to talk.

He asked the day of the week as well as various other questions which were answered for him. Finally Nancy walked over to the table. Picking up Miss Judson's photograph, she handed it to the sick man.

"Would you like to have me place this picture near you where you can see it?" she inquired gently.

"Yes, please do," Mr. Haley answered in faltering tones. "Miss Margaret—isn't she here now?"

"Miss Judson has never come to the cabin. She does not know that you have been ill."

"Then it was a dream—I thought she was sitting beside me, holding my hand."

"Perhaps you confused me with Miss Judson," Nancy said quietly. "Tell me, did you work for her at the old mansion?"

"Oh, yes, I took care of the trees and the garden and the flowers about the place. I was employed by the Judsons for nearly ten years. After Miss Margaret's parents died she didn't have as much money as before, but she kept me there just the same."

A tear glistened in Mr. Haley's eye as he thought of the happy years which were no more. Several moments elapsed before he spoke again.

"Miss Margaret was good and kind," he told his listeners. "She never once spoke a harsh word to me in all the years I knew her. That's why it hurt me to see her so unhappy."

"Miss Judson was very unhappy?" Nancy prompted as the old man fell into another meditative silence.

"Yes. After her parents died she was very lonely. She was to have been married, but the awful fire came and all her plans were changed."

"In what way do you mean?" Carson Drew inquired, leaning eagerly toward the bed.

"I don't know—" Mr. Haley murmured wearily. "Something happened—I never learned just what it was. Miss Margaret was greatly upset about the fire. She ran away."

"And you have never seen her since?" Nancy questioned softly.

"She came back to my cabin once to ask me to search for something she had lost. But I couldn't find it. I hunted everywhere. I told her that later and she never came again."

Mr. Haley closed his eyes and turned his face toward the wall. Nancy and her father longed to ask him other questions but they dared not, cognizant of the fact that the old man was spent from his efforts at speaking.

"I want to see Miss Margaret," he mumbled feebly a few minutes later. Then he dropped off into a sound slumber.

Before Carson Drew and Nancy could discuss the information Mr. Haley had given them, Ned, Bud and Bill came into the bedroom.

"We're ready to leave, Nancy," Ned announced in a whisper. "How do you like my new suit?"

"You look handsome in it," Nancy praised, without noting in detail what he wore. "I'll get my hat and coat."

As the young people were leaving the cabin together, Ned observed that his companion was strangely silent.

"Don't you feel well tonight, Nancy?" he inquired anxiously.

"There's really nothing wrong with me, Ned. I was just thinking——"

"Not about that fellow Mortimer, I hope?"

Nancy laughed as she shook her head. "No, I happened to be wondering about Margaret Judson again. Ned, I *must* find her!"

"That's easier said than done."

"Yes, but I believe she is somewhere near here."

Ned glanced curiously at Nancy. Her next words astonished him even more, for with a quiet intensity in her voice she added:

"It may sound silly to you, Ned, but I have a strange feeling—call it intuition if you will. Tonight I *know* I shall find Miss Judson!"

CHAPTER XXI

The Note in the Fountain

"You seem very positive that you'll locate Margaret Judson," Ned commented with a teasing smile. "I thought you didn't believe in hunches, Nancy."

"Well, in a way I don't," the girl confessed. "But somehow this feeling I have is so strong I can't ignore it. Something tells me I'll meet the woman before the evening is over."

"I certainly hope your hunch is right, because you've been worrying about her ever since you came to the Deer Mountain Hotel."

"I'm afraid I've been ruining everyone else's pleasure with my own selfish problems."

"Your problems are not selfish ones," Ned replied quickly. "I know how important it is that Miss Judson be located."

"Are you willing to help me?" Nancy asked eagerly.

"Of course. I thought you didn't need my assistance."

"Oh, Ned, it was just that I couldn't explain everything, and I'm afraid I can't even now."

"That doesn't matter, Nancy. You tell me

what to do and I'll obey orders with no questions asked.''

"It may mean ruining your evening, Ned. Are you willing to substitute sleuthing for dancing?"

"We can dance when we get back to River Heights."

"That's the way I feel about it," Nancy agreed in satisfaction. "It may be that I am too hopeful, but I honestly believe matters will come to a climax tonight."

Meanwhile, at the Deer Mountain Hotel George and Bess were wondering what had become of their chum. They had not seen her since the start of the golf match and could not imagine where she might be.

"I didn't mean to worry you," Nancy apologized on arriving as she greeted her chums. "I merely jumped from one thing to another so fast that it didn't occur to me to leave word where I was going to be."

Bess and George were enthusiastic regarding plans for the dance, and promptly forgave Nancy the anxiety she had caused them. Then they hastened to their room to change into evening frocks. Ned, Bill and Bud stayed in the lobby as Nancy went to the desk to inquire for mail.

The clerk handed her two envelopes, one of them plain, the other bearing the stamp of the hotel. Nancy decided instantly that the latter was from Mortimer Bartescue, for the handwriting was similar to one of the specimens of his which she had collected. She opened it and read:

"I won my golf match today and hope that rain did not cause you to lose yours. Important business calls me away from the hotel for a few days, but I hope to see you again before you return to your home."

"Important business," Nancy mused as she tucked the letter into her pocket. "I wonder if it concerns Miss Judson!"

She opened the second letter, and was astonished to learn that it was from the very person whose name had been in her thoughts.

The brief message read:

"The bearer who takes this note to your hotel has said that you wish to see me. Please write your message and leave it tonight before nine o'clock in the hand of the fountain statue. Margaret Judson."

Nancy read the note a second time to be certain that she gathered its amazing contents, then turned to the desk clerk.

"Can you tell me who brought this letter to the hotel?" she queried.

"I was not on duty at the time, Miss Drew."

Nancy wondered if the messenger could have been Bartescue. There seemed no way to find

this out until the day clerk should resume his
duties at the hotel. She quickly sought Ned
and showed him the note.

"I can't understand how Miss Judson learned
that I wished to see her, unless it was through
Mortimer Bartescue."

"Well, at least it looks as if your sense of
intuition is correct, Nancy. You may meet
Margaret Judson before the evening is over."

"I told you I would!" the girl laughed gaily.
"Ned, let's walk into the garden. I want to
look around. I'm not certain which statue Miss
Judson means."

"I'd say it was the large one at the rear of
the hotel. Isn't that the only statue connected
with a fountain?"

Nancy could recall no other, but she wanted
to make certain. Without appearing to be
particularly interested in the surroundings, the
couple walked slowly about the hotel grounds.
Finally they halted by the fountain, pretending
to watch the goldfish in the basin around it.

"You're apt to get wet if you try to place a
note in the hand of this statue!" Ned chuckled
softly. "Will you carry out the orders,
Nancy?"

"I intend to leave a blank sheet of paper
here, Ned. I would write a note but I'm not
certain Miss Judson sent me that letter."

"You think it's a forgery?"

"It could be. I'd like to compare Miss Judson's signature with the one which appears on

Mr. Haley's photograph, but I won't have time now to go back to the cabin.''

Ned looked at his watch. "No, I guess you won't, for it's very nearly nine o'clock."

"We must work quickly. First, I'll get a blank sheet of paper. Wait here, Ned."

Nancy ran back into the hotel, soon reappearing with a folded envelope in her hand. Seating themselves on a nearby bench the couple waited until the grounds were deserted. Ned then leaned across the stone basin of the fountain and placed the sheet of paper in the hand of the marble figure.

"Now we'll act as if we're returning to the hotel," Nancy whispered. "We'll steal back here and keep watch to see if anyone comes for the message."

They retraced their steps to the hotel, walked directly through the lobby, and left by a side entrance. Selecting a bench which was screened from the fountain by high bushes, they stationed themselves to wait. Nine o'clock came, and from within the hotel Nancy and Ned heard the first strains of the orchestra as it tuned up for the dance.

"I'll gladly wait here alone," Nancy offered as she saw her companion glance wistfully toward the lighted ballroom. "Won't you go inside and dance?"

"No, I'd rather stay here with you," he insisted.

Nine-thirty arrived, but still no one had come

to retrieve the message. Shortly before ten o'clock a couple strolled near the fountain, but after lingering there for a few minutes, walked on again.

"Oh, it's useless to wait," Nancy declared at last. "We've wasted an hour already."

"I'm willing to stay here if you want me to," Ned offered generously.

"No, I'm beginning to think that the note will never be claimed. Ned, will you do me another favor?"

"You know I will, Nancy."

"This may sound like a silly request, but I'd like to have you drive me over to Hemlock Hall in your car."

"I'll be glad to do it. It's such a warm night that a ride will be more fun than dancing."

Nancy was convinced by this time that she could not hope to meet Margaret Judson at the Deer Mountain Hotel. She suspected that the note requesting her to leave a message in the hand of the statue had been written by Mortimer Bartescue, who doubtless hoped to obtain information in that manner.

"Haven't you searched for Miss Judson in the Hemlock Hall vicinity before?" Ned questioned curiously as he and Nancy drove away.

"Yes, several times, but tonight I have a new idea. It occurred to me that she may have rented a home near the hotel. I want to interview various real estate agents."

"Their offices will be closed, Nancy."

"I know, but we'll call at their homes. Oh, Ned, I *must* find Miss Judson tonight!"

"We'll not leave a stone unturned," the young man promised. "We'll search until dawn if necessary."

Nancy and Ned set forth with high hopes to visit every real estate agent in the little city of Mapleton, which was the one nearest to Hemlock Hall. They met nothing but discouragement, and only their grim determination not to give up drove them on. Finally, on interviewing the last real estate man on their list, they met with a favorable response.

"Why yes," the agent reported, "I rented a house only this morning to a strange young woman. I believe her name was Judson, but I can't tell for sure without examining my records."

When Nancy had assured him that the matter was of vital importance the realtor obligingly agreed to accompany the couple to his office. There he found his real estate files, and to the girl's delight confirmed his previous recollection.

"Yes, I was correct. The house at 508 Elmwood street was taken by a woman named Margaret Judson. She asked for a six months' lease."

Nancy thanked the man for his trouble. Writing down the address, she hurried back to the car with Ned. The real estate agent had given them precise directions for reaching Elmwood street so they had no difficulty in locating a large white house which bore the number 508. However, Nancy was disappointed to find it in darkness.

"Perhaps Miss Judson has gone to bed," Ned suggested, halting the car on the opposite side of the street.

"I'm inclined to think she hasn't moved in yet, Ned."

"Well, I guess there's nothing more we can do tonight. I'll run across the street and try the bell if you like, but it's a good guess no one is at home."

He started to open the car door, but Nancy suddenly placed a restraining hand on his arm.

"Wait!" she commanded tensely.

A car with brilliant headlights came slowly down the street, and the woman driver appeared to be studying each house in turn. She swung into the gravel driveway at number 508.

"That must be Miss Judson now!" Nancy said excitedly. "We'll wait here, Ned, until she enters the house, and then we'll knock!"

They watched a shadowy figure leave the auto and disappear inside the building by a side door. Almost at once the lower floor was flooded with light. The window shades were lowered.

"Shall we go now?" Nancy suggested excitedly.

The couple presented themselves at the front door, groping about in the darkness for an electric bell button. Presently they heard footsteps.

"Here she comes now," Nancy whispered nervously. "If she should prove to be Miss Judson, we won't tell her the real purpose of our visit."

The door opened, and the same young woman whom Nancy had met at Hemlock Hall peered out at the pair. She failed to recognize the girl, and decided that the two were representatives of a real estate firm. She started to explain that she no longer was interested in buying or renting a house, then stopped in confusion as she realized she had mistaken the identity of her callers.

"Oh, now I remember you," she said to Nancy as a beam of light fell directly on the girl's face. "We met at Hemlock Hall. Do come in, and please excuse the condition of this house for I am just moving in."

"You are Margaret Judson, if I am not mistaken," Nancy began cautiously as she and Ned seated themselves.

"Yes," the young woman smiled.

"I have rather distressing news to report," Nancy continued. "While staying at the Deer Mountain Hotel I became acquainted with an old man who formerly worked at your estate."

"Not Joe Haley?" the woman asked quickly. "He is well?"

"Quite the contrary. Mr. Haley has been injured in an accident, and for days he has remained practically unconscious. He has talked of you constantly and keeps pleading that you come to see him.''

"Oh, I must go to him at once!" Miss Judson cried. "You must take me to the hospital!"

"Mr. Haley is still at his cabin in the woods," Nancy explained. "The doctor did not think it advisable to move him."

"Then I shall go there, of course. I'll get my hat and purse."

In her anxiety Miss Judson could not find the articles though they were lying on a table in plain view. Ned placed them in her hands. Suddenly a startled expression came over the young woman's face.

"No, I can't go after all," she murmured. "It will be impossible."

"Why do you hesitate to visit Mr. Haley?" Nancy asked gently. "He needs you."

"I want to go—you don't understand. I am afraid I might meet a certain person there."

"Morton Wardell?" Nancy Drew questioned softly.

Margaret Judson flung herself on a sofa. Burying her face in her hands, she sobbed wildly.

"Yes, yes, he is the one. I can never face him as long as I am accused of being a thief!"

CHAPTER XXII

The Chums' Help

While Nancy and Ned were many miles away, Bess, George and their escorts were enjoying the dance at the Deer Mountain Hotel.

"The party soon will be over," Bess declared anxiously as she gazed about the ballroom. "What can be keeping Nancy?"

"Ned was eager to attend this dance, too," Bill Cowan added. "It's queer he disappeared."

"I imagine they're both out in the garden," George suggested. "Let's look there."

"I've already been outside," Bess replied soberly. "I'm beginning to be worried."

Before she could say more, a page boy came through the ballroom, calling George Fayne's name. The girls summoned him, hoping that Nancy had sent a note to explain her absence.

"You are wanted at the telephone, Miss Fayne," the page told George.

"I can't imagine who would call me here," the girl murmured in perplexity. "I don't believe it's from Nancy. It might be from home."

The girl's guess was entirely correct. Mrs. Fayne in River Heights, lonesome for the sound of her daughter's voice, had telephoned merely to inquire if she were all right.

"Oh, yes, Mother," George replied eagerly. "We're having a grand time here. I intended to write more often—but you know how it is."

"Yes, I know," Mrs. Fayne laughed. "I want you to have a nice vacation so that you'll come home rested and ready for school."

"School," George answered with a grimace which her mother could not see. "I hate even to think of it. How is Dad?"

"Oh, just as well as ever, George. But I have some bad news for you. One of your pet kittens has been sick and we're afraid it will die——"

At this point George lost the thread of conversation completely, for in the adjoining booth she heard the excited voice of a man saying into the telephone:

"So the fellow was a forger! He skipped out! That is a shock, for he had good references!"

"Did you hear what I said?" Mrs. Fayne questioned her daughter anxiously. "Your pet kitten——"

"Oh, yes, that's nice," George replied hastily, her mind upon the conversation in the next booth.

"Those two B-A-R's look alike?" she heard the man ask. "And you say the M and the T are similar? Yes, I agree that ought to be enough to convict him."

George's mind worked with lightning-like speed. Undoubtedly the letters B-A-R- came from the first part of Mortimer Bartescue's surname while the M had been taken from his given name. The man was a forger just as Nancy had suspected! Very likely the person in the next booth was one of the hotel officials just being told of the discovery.

"George," came her mother's voice in exasperation, "what is the matter with you? Can't you hear what I am saying or are you really glad your kitten is ill?"

"Oh, yes—I mean, no—" George stammered. "I hear what you are saying, but something important has come up. I can't talk now. I'll call back a little later."

She hastily hung up the receiver and darted from the phone booth. Even so, she was too late to learn who had occupied the adjoining one for it was now empty.

"Nancy will want to know this latest information about Bartescue," she told herself excitedly. "I must find her."

Since her chum was not available, she sought Bess, making a pretext to draw her into the garden.

"I've just made an important discovery," she revealed to her chum. "Mortimer Bartescue is a forger and apparently the hotel people are looking for him!"

"No wonder he skipped out!" Bess exclaimed indignantly. "That explains the note he left for Nancy. The man probably is miles from here by now."

"I'm afraid of it. But he is supposed to play his final golf match tomorrow. Let's walk down to the caddy house and learn if his clubs are gone."

"It isn't likely he'd consider returning for a golf match—not when it might mean a prison sentence."

"Well, let's find out anyway. It will take only a minute."

The girls walked across the grounds toward the caddy house, plainly outlined in the moonlight. The shack had been locked for the night. Disappointed, they turned back to the hotel.

Suddenly Bess noticed a bright object gleaming at her feet in the grass. She stooped and picked it up.

"Someone dropped his keys, George."

"One of the golfers, I imagine. We can turn the ring in at the office."

Bess dropped the keys into her pocket, and they walked on toward the hotel. As they came within view of the garden, George abruptly halted, clutching her cousin's arm.

"Bess, look toward that statue by the fountain!"

"Mortimer Bartescue!"

"What in the world is he trying to do? Steal the goldfish?"

The girls crept forward, taking care to keep themselves screened by bushes and trees which were between them and the man. They saw him reach across the basin of the fountain and remove a white object from the hand of the statue.

"What did he do that for?" Bess whispered in wonder.

"It must have been a note from someone," George replied in an undertone. "Bess, we must capture that man—he is a forger, wanted by the police."

"We can't do anything alone."

"No, we must steal back to the hotel and get Bill and Bud. There's not a second to lose!"

Quietly the girls hurried away. Finding their escorts in the ballroom, they poured forth their exciting story. Bud and Bill, always ready for an adventure, were eager to help.

"Perhaps we should notify the hotel people," Bess suggested, but the boys shook their heads.

"We can handle that fellow alone," they insisted. "Come on, let's get him!"

The four let themselves out by a side entrance, and quietly approached the fountain. Mortimer Bartescue was standing there, studying a sheet of paper in his hand. They heard him mutter something, whereupon he crumpled the paper and hurled it angrily into the fountain.

"Now is our chance!" Bud whispered. "We'll sneak up from behind and grab him!"

The boys moved stealthily forward, but the moonlight was bright, and just at that moment Mortimer Bartescue turned his head. He gave a cry of alarm and fled toward the caddy house.

"Don't let him get away!" Bud cried as the four young people gave chase.

Bill, who was a champion sprinter on a college track team, soon overtook the man, throwing him to the ground. Bud and the girls closed in so that Bartescue had no chance to escape.

"What is the meaning of this outrage?" the fellow demanded furiously. "Let me up."

"We'll let you up when the police come," Bill retorted grimly. "You low-down forger!"

"I've never forged anything in my life," Bartescue denied in a rasping tone. "Let me up or you'll pay for this."

Bill and Bud paid not the slightest heed to the man's protestations. However, they discovered that it was not easy to keep Bartescue confined, for he was strong and agile.

Bess glanced quickly toward the caddy house. Inspired by a sudden thought, she ran to the locked door to try the various keys which she had found only a few minutes before. To her delight one of them fit perfectly and she was able to unlock the door.

Bartescue was thrust roughly into the caddy house and the door securely locked again. Bill and Bud said they would stand guard while the girls ran back to the hotel to notify the officials.

"Let me out of here!" Bartescue yelled at the top of his lungs, pounding savagely on the door. "You have no right to do this! What have I done?"

"Plenty!" Bud told him through the barred window. "Besides being accused of forgery, you're a thief."

"You've stolen money from widows and orphans," Bill went on glibly. "You're also wanted for house-breaking. Oh, you'll be lucky if you don't get a life sentence!"

"There's some terrible mistake," Bartescue moaned. "I've done none of these things. Get me a lawyer."

"You'll have one soon enough," Bill told him grimly. "Just wait until the police get here."

In the meantime Bess and George had reached the hotel. Laboring under great excitement they hurried to the manager's office, bursting in upon the man as he was conferring with another hotel official.

"Come quickly!" George cried. "We've captured your forger!"

"What?" the manager demanded incredulously, springing up from his chair. "You have caught the man?"

"Yes, we have him—in the caddy house!" So great was George's excitement that she began to stammer. "F-follow us."

Bess and George were fairly glowing with pride by the time they came to the caddy house. All was quiet within, for Mortimer Bartescue finally had decided that it was useless to try to convince the boys of his innocence. He had collapsed in a corner of the room and was moaning softly. Bess unlocked the door and the manager cautiously peered inside.

"Come out of there, you!" he ordered sharply. "Get a move on or we'll drag you out!"

Mussed and disheveled, Mortimer Bartescue haughtily emerged from the building. He glared at Bess and George before bestowing an accusing glance upon the hotel official.

"Sir, I demand an explanation for this outrageous treatment. Never before in all my life have I been so abused and insulted! Rest assured I shall take this matter to the courts!"

The manager had spoken no word. He could only stare.

"Oh, Mr. Bartescue, a thousand pardons," the man murmured at last. "This is all a mistake."

"A mistake!" George exclaimed indignantly. "Why, this man is a forger. I heard you say so yourself when you were talking in a telephone booth. Or at least I thought it was you."

"Yes, yes, I recall the conversation. But it is not Mortimer Bartescue who is wanted for forgery."

"But the letters—B-A-R——"

"They stand for Barney. One of our newly employed cooks, a man by the name of Jennings, forged a hundred dollar check, putting on it the signature of Barney Martin, who is our caddy master. Mr. Bartescue had nothing whatever to do with the matter.''

"Oh, then I've made a dreadful mistake,'' George murmured in confusion. "I shouldn't have acted so impulsively, only I thought Mr. Bartescue was under suspicion even before this. He has written his name so many different ways.''

"I can explain that,'' Bartescue said coldly.

"Then please do,'' Bess pleaded. "I am sure it would clear up a great deal of mis-understanding.''

"I shall explain nothing to you,'' the man retorted rudely. "When Miss Drew comes I will reveal everything to her—in private!''

Haughtily the man turned and walked toward the hotel. The manager and his companion hastened after him, continuing to offer apologies for the mistake which had been made.

"I seem to have achieved the prize blunder,'' George murmured contritely. "I acted too quickly.''

"I'm afraid we all did,'' Bess agreed soberly. "But the fact remains that Bartescue still has a lot to explain.''

"We must find Nancy immediately,'' George declared urgently. "Mr. Bartescue may slip away, and then we'll never learn the reason for his strange actions.''

CHAPTER XXIII

An Exoneration

Following Margaret Judson's plaintive declaration that she could not face her former fiance, Morton Wardell, because of the charge of theft which stood against her, Nancy sought to draw from the young woman the story of her troubles.

"You are innocent of the accusation?" she inquired gently.

"Oh, yes, yes. I have never misappropriated anything in my life."

Miss Judson was embarrassed to have revealed so much, but finding Nancy kind and sympathetic, she tried to explain the difficulties of her situation.

"It happened years ago," she related. "I had been abroad and was returning on a French liner. Enroute home I met a charming woman named Mrs. Brownell and we became good friends. I finally invited her to spend a weekend at my home."

"The house near the Deer Mountain Hotel?" Nancy interposed.

"Yes, I was living there at the time. Mrs.

189

Brownell accepted my invitation. One evening, learning that my guest loved beautiful jewelry, I opened the safe and showed her a box of family heirlooms. Instead of returning it to the vault as I should have done, I carelessly placed the container in my bureau drawer.

"Later that night as I was preparing for bed, Mrs. Brownell came to my room to show me a jeweled vanity case. It was an exquisite piece, as lovely as anything I have ever seen. We chatted for a time, and then my visitor went back to her room, leaving the vanity case on my dresser."

"You did not attempt to return it to her?" Nancy inquired in surprise.

"She had retired before I noticed that she had overlooked it. I meant to give it to her early in the morning. You probably can guess the rest of the tale."

"Fire broke out during the night?"

"Yes, it seemed to be everywhere at once. When I awoke, the bedroom was filled with smoke, and flames were shooting up the stairway. I ran to Mrs. Brownell's room and after awakening her aroused the servants. By then it was too late to save very much, and we were all forced to escape down a porch trellis."

"Did you forget the box of jewelry?" Nancy questioned.

"No, I wrapped it in some of my clothing, snatched up Mrs. Brownell's vanity case and my pocketbook, and managed to escape just an instant before the floor of my room crashed. In terror I ran toward old Joe Haley's cabin, intending to ask him to guard the jewelry.

"Somehow I became lost. Later I remembered that I had stumbled across the ravine bridge, but about what happened after that my memory isn't very clear. Apparently I wandered through the woods until I fainted. In any event, hours elapsed before I recovered consciousness. I was chilled to the bone."

"The experience must have been a frightful one," Nancy murmured sympathetically.

"I can never forget it—never. When I looked about, the bundle of clothing and my pocketbook were still beside me. The little casket of jewelry and Mrs. Brownell's vanity case were gone."

"Did you notice footprints near by?" Nancy interposed quickly.

Miss Judson shook her head. "I was too excited to notice anything. I wandered about in a semi-dazed condition, hoping I'd find the jewelry. I felt certain I had dropped it somewhere in the woods.

"When dawn came I knew that the search was useless. I staggered to Mr. Haley's cabin and told him I had lost the jewelry. I begged him to help me find it. He promised he would."

"The jewelry represented a great loss?" Ned inquired, for he had never seen the contents of the carved brass chest.

"Yes, several of the pieces were priceless.

Among the articles was my diamond engagement ring, which I valued above all else. And of course Mrs. Brownell's vanity case was worth a small fortune."

"According to her estimate?" Nancy inquired with a smile.

"Yes, she claimed it was valued at three thousand dollars. And she blamed me entirely for the loss."

"How could she do that when she had left the article on your bureau?" Ned asked. "She was lucky that it didn't burn."

"Perhaps you were unwise to let her know that you had saved the piece for her," Nancy added quietly.

"I never told her," Miss Judson confessed. "Mrs. Brownell gave me no opportunity. She had followed me to Joe Haley's cabin and overheard me tell him that I had recovered the vanity case. She demanded that I return it immediately or pay her three thousand dollars."

"That was gratitude for you!" Ned commented. "I'd have told her to go jump in the ravine!"

"I had thought Mrs. Brownell to be a very charming person," Miss Judson continued, "but I learned to my sorrow that I knew nothing of her true character. She threatened to turn me over to the police. I gladly would have paid the three thousand dollars but I could not afford to. Nearly everything I owned except a few acres of land had been destroyed in the fire.''

"I do not believe that any court would have substantiated the woman's claim," Nancy said thoughtfully. "Probably she was only trying to frighten you.''

"You mean she couldn't have caused my arrest?''

"I think not, Miss Judson.''

"She would have claimed that I had hidden the jewel case deliberately.''

"Even so, Mrs. Brownell could not win her case without proof. You should have consulted a lawyer.''

"I realize that now, but at the time I was panic-stricken. I ran away, living for a time in Chicago.''

"That was the very worst thing you could have done," Ned assured her. "Flight tended to confirm your guilt.''

"I was so upset I acted impulsively. I kept hoping that Joe Haley would find the jewel chest, for I felt certain it was somewhere in the woods. So many years have elapsed now, that of course the search is useless.''

"Perhaps not," Nancy remarked quietly, but the young woman did not seem to hear her.

"Mrs. Brownell has never ceased to bother me since the vanity case was lost," Miss Judson went on. "While she has never come to me herself, she sends a friend.''

"A friend?" Nancy inquired alertly.

"Another woman, who follows me wherever I go. She keeps pressing me for money and threatening that unless I pay she will expose me to my friends and to the police. I am at my wits' end, Miss Drew—I'd rather be dead than be subjected to this torment all my life."

"Miss Judson, I think your troubles are very nearly at an end," Nancy said kindly. "Your jewel box has been found."

Miss Judson sprang from the sofa, trembling with eagerness.

"Did Joe Haley tell you that? He found my casket?"

"No, it came into my possession by accident," Nancy explained. "Tell me, what was the little chest made of?"

"Carved brass, and the design was very beautiful. I can't describe it, but I can give you some idea of it by a drawing."

Seizing a pencil, Miss Judson made a rough sketch which convinced Nancy beyond any doubt that the chest she had found in the ravine belonged to the young woman.

"Tell me, did it contain the missing vanity case?" Margaret Judson asked anxiously.

"Yes, and the diamond ring you mentioned. I think everything is there as it was on the night of the fire."

"Oh, Miss Drew, how can I ever thank you? This means everything to me for now I can go to old Joe Haley, and—and I'll not be afraid to face Morton."

"We'll drive to the cabin if you wish," Nancy offered. "Mr. Haley will be very happy to see you again."

As the car sped along the road toward the Deer Mountain locality, Nancy answered the young woman's many questions concerning the manner in which the carved chest had been found.

"Could I have dropped it on the bank of the stream when I crossed the bridge the night of the fire?" she speculated. "I have no recollection of anything I did."

"It is quite possible the chest slipped from the bundle of clothing you had put it in," Nancy agreed thoughtfully. "I found it buried deep in the mud."

Leaving the automobile parked by the roadside, the three walked along the trail to the cabin. From a distance they could see lights glimmering through the trees. As they approached closer they heard men's voices. Nancy assumed that her father was talking with Mr. Haley, and she felt elated to think that the patient was gaining steadily in strength.

The sound of footsteps brought Carson Drew to the door. As he flung it open, Nancy glanced inquiringly at Miss Judson, for she saw that her father had a visitor. Directly behind him stood Morton Wardell.

CHAPTER XXIV

A Detective's Invitation

Miss Judson failed to see her former fiance until after she had entered the lighted cabin. Then, as their eyes met in a startled glance, neither spoke for an instant. An awkward silence fell. Even Nancy could think of nothing to say or do in such a crisis. At last Morton Wardell took a step toward the young woman, his hand outstretched.

"Margaret," he murmured brokenly.

"Morton," she responded, and with a little sob threw herself into his arms. "I have missed you so much. And our separation was all a mistake, a dreadful mistake."

Mr. Drew, Nancy and Ned felt that they had no right to witness the happy reunion. They slipped quietly into the adjoining bedroom, using the pretext that they wished to see Mr. Haley.

"If we just allow them to talk everything over alone, I'm sure matters will adjust themselves quickly," Nancy whispered to her father.

"This plan of yours to reunite the lovers is all very well," Carson Drew returned gravely, "but you seem to forget the charge against Miss Judson. I was assigned to work on the jewel-theft case and I can't allow my sympathy——"

Nancy laughingly pressed her fingers against her father's lips.

"Don't say another word, Dad, until you've heard my story. Margaret Judson is absolutely innocent. She has explained everything to my complete satisfaction."

"Perhaps not to mine," Mr. Drew rejoined with a trace of amusement. "By any chance, did Miss Judson identify the various members of the international jewel-theft gang?"

"Not intentionally, but she gave me a splendid clue. I'll tell you the entire story."

With a word now and then from Ned, Nancy repeated all that she had learned from Miss Judson, and was gratified to observe that the information seemed to impress her father.

"In my opinion, Mrs. Brownell and her mysterious friend are the suspicious persons in the case," she ended by saying. "They must be the criminal type or they would not have attempted to extort money from Miss Judson."

Carson Drew nodded. "You may be right, Nancy, for the jeweled vanity case positively was identified by New York police as stolen property."

There was no opportunity to say more just then, for the door opened to admit Miss Judson and Morton Wardell. Both were smiling, and they did not need to announce that the old engagement had been renewed.

"I'll never be able to repay you for your kindness," the young woman told Nancy, tears gleaming in her eyes. "Ask any favor——"

"I have just one, Miss Judson. I want you to talk with my father about Mrs. Brownell and her friend, and give him any information which you may have concerning either of them."

"It is so little to ask. I'll be only too glad to answer all your questions."

Mr. Haley, who had been sleeping soundly, stirred restlessly, and Nancy stepped forward to remove the screen which shielded his bed Miss Judson took the old man's hand in her own, kneeling beside him as she did so.

"Is that you—Miss Margaret?" he whispered.

"Yes, it is I," she answered softly. "You must try to get well. You'll do it for my sake, won't you?"

"Yes," the old man murmured, his eyes roving over her lovely face. "I am so glad you have come. But I have failed you again. I tried, but I couldn't find the box."

"It doesn't matter now, Joe. The chest has been found. You are not to worry about it any more."

With a sigh of relief the old man closed his eyes and within a few minutes had fallen again into a restful sleep. While Ned remained at the bedside, Mr. Drew and Nancy took Miss

Judson into the kitchen, there to question her regarding Mrs. Brownell.

"I have no idea what became of the woman," Miss Judson reported, "but her friend annoyed me a few days ago at Hemlock Hall. I think she is staying at one of the local hotels now."

"Could you get in touch with her by to-morrow?" Mr. Drew asked.

"I suppose so," the other answered reluctantly.

Deciding to take the young woman into his confidence, Carson Drew explained why he wished to locate Mrs. Brownell and her accomplice. Miss Judson promised that she would do everything in her power to cooperate with the law.

"If you are able to locate this person, tell her you have recovered the jewelry," Mr. Drew instructed. "Ask her to meet you here at this cabin if she wishes to receive the lost vanity case."

"I'm almost afraid to see the woman alone," Miss Judson answered reluctantly. "She has a violent temper."

"Perhaps I could go with you," Nancy suggested eagerly, adding in disappointment, "Oh, I forgot about the golf tournament to-morrow."

"I believe I can arrange matters for you so that your match can be played in the afternoon," Mr. Drew smiled. "The tournament chairman is a very reasonable man."

A few minutes later, Miss Judson, her fiance, Nancy and Mr. Drew prepared to motor back to the Deer Mountain Hotel.

"As usual, you seem to be the one who must hold the fort," Nancy said to Ned as she told him good-bye. "After this case is settled, we'll try to have some good times."

"I enjoyed myself tonight," Ned told her truthfully. "I haven't had so much excitement in a year."

At the hotel Nancy found her worried chums. After she had sent Bud and Bill back to the cabin to keep Ned company she helped settle Miss Judson in a room not far from her own. At the young woman's request she lingered for a few minutes to talk.

"There is a question that I should like to ask you," Nancy ventured.

"Certainly. What is it?"

"I don't wish to seem personal, but are you well acquainted with a man named Mortimer Bartescue?"

"Why, no," Miss Judson replied promptly. "I met him on my trip abroad, but I can't say that I liked him very well."

"Have you seen him since your return to this country?"

"Oh, no, he was just a casual acquaintance."

"Mr. Bartescue has been staying at this hotel," Nancy explained. "He pretended to know you well, but I half suspected he was only bluffing."

"I believe Mrs. Brownell knew the man," Miss Judson said thoughtfully. "It was through her that I met him, and she often mentioned his name."

"Did you consider Mr. Bartescue to be an honest person?"

"Why yes, I have never heard that he was otherwise."

Miss Judson's eyes were heavy. Suspecting that the young woman wished to retire, Nancy soon said goodnight and returned to the room of her chums. Bess and George eagerly awaited her, and almost before the door had closed, bombarded her with questions. In turn they related their own adventure with Mortimer Bartescue.

"Don't feel bad about your mistake, George," Nancy chuckled. "It served the man right. He thought he would play a grand joke on me by asking me to leave a message in the hand of the statue."

"I still think he must be a crook," George insisted gloomily. "Otherwise, how do you explain all those different signatures?"

"I suspect the man is a practical joker. I'll try to talk with him tomorrow and find out."

In the morning Nancy learned from the tournament chairman that her golf match had been postponed until two o'clock. That left her ample time to go with Miss Judson to Hemlock Hall, where she believed Mrs. Brownell's friend had engaged a room.

"She calls herself Mrs. Martlett," the young woman explained as she and Nancy drove toward the hotel in Mr. Drew's car. "However, I think that is not her true name."

Learning that the woman was still at Hemlock Hall, Miss Judson went to a house phone and requested Mrs. Martlett to meet her in the lobby. Nancy then stationed herself within hearing distance, but in such a position that she would not be noticed.

Soon a woman emerged from the elevator, walking directly toward Miss Judson. Nancy instantly recognized her as the same person who had worn a flowered dress upon the night she had visited Hemlock Hall with Mortimer Bartescue. The conversation between the two was brief, ending when Mrs. Martlett promised to come to the cabin in the woods directly after luncheon, bringing Mrs. Brownell with her.

"Everything is moving smoothly according to Dad's plan," Nancy declared in delight when she and Margaret Judson were leaving the hotel together. "I only hope my golf match won't keep me from witnessing the grand finale."

"If we have a few minutes, I'd like to stop at my house and pick up a few clothes," her companion said. "I really have nothing at the Deer Mountain Hotel, and I'd like to dress up a bit."

"For Morton?" Nancy asked teasingly.

"Yes," the young woman admitted, blushing. "I feel very gay and I'd like to dress the part."

"I don't blame you," Nancy responded, but she added soberly, "I hope everything turns out as well as we expect."

Margaret Judson glanced at her in quick alarm. "Surely you don't think I'll not be cleared of the charges against me?"

"Oh, I'm hoping things will adjust themselves," Nancy answered hastily, not wishing to alarm the young woman.

"I don't see how anything can go wrong now."

Nancy did not reply, but it occurred to her that if Mrs. Brownell should secure the slightest inkling that she was under suspicion, the woman would not keep the appointment at Mr. Haley's cabin.

It was luncheon time when the pair reached the Deer Mountain Hotel. As soon as she had snatched a bite to eat, Nancy hastened to meet Miss Howard on the golf course. In crossing the lawn she encountered Mortimer Bartescue, who had just finished his final match. From the expression on his face she gathered that he had lost the men's championship.

"How did you come out in your game?" she questioned carelessly.

"I lost," the man snapped. "I blame it on those two chums of yours, too!"

"What did they have to do with it?"

"I was so upset by everything that happened

last night I couldn't get a grip on myself. My swing was badly off."

"That's too bad," Nancy replied evenly. "Mistakes will happen."

As she tried to walk on, Mortimer Bartescue attached himself to her, seemingly eager to talk.

"Last night I told your friends I'd explain everything to you and to you only," he declared.

"Yes?" Nancy inquired.

"I've known from the first that you are Nancy Drew."

"Why shouldn't you have known it? I made no mystery of my name."

"I mean, I was aware that you are the famous Nancy Drew, known far and wide for your ability as a detective."

"You exaggerate, I fear."

"I made up my mind to match my wits with yours," Bartescue went on. "I guess I fooled you too, didn't I?"

"For a few days," Nancy answered coldly. "But I suspected the truth long before you thought I did."

"About my handwriting?" the man asked, looking crestfallen.

"Yes, you changed your signature a bit too often. It was too obvious that you were intending to bewilder me."

"I guess maybe I wasn't quite as smart as I thought then. But I did have you running around in circles for a time. Years ago when I was in college I discovered that I had a talent for imitating handwriting, and I've had a lot of fun doing it ever since.''

"I'd advise you to give up the pastime or you may yet find yourself in trouble with the law," Nancy said severely. "The next time it may not be so easy to prove yourself innocent of charges of forgery against you.''

"Oh, I can take care of myself,'' the man chuckled. "Well, young lady, run along since you seem to be in such a hurry. After you win your match we'll have tea together and I'll buy you a 2 B X gardenia!''

Laughing heartily at his own joke, he walked on toward the hotel.

"We'll *not* have tea together,'' Nancy muttered furiously to herself. "The conceit of that man! I've never met anyone like him in all my life, and I hope I may never see him again!''

Try as she would, the girl could not calm her ruffled feelings, and she was still angry as she met her opponent. With Miss Howard she walked to the fifteenth tee where play was to be resumed. A large gallery had followed the two players and Nancy's chums had joined the crowd.

It was generally conceded that Miss Howard should win the match, for in being one point ahead with only four holes left to play, she held a great advantage. Then, too, it was known that Nancy's hand had been injured and few persons believed that she could play her best game with such a handicap.

Miss Howard, who held the honor of driving first, sent a long, straight ball flying down the fairway. Undaunted, Nancy teed up her ball and while the gallery stood a-tiptoe, swung her club with all her strength. With only four holes to play she had no intention of babying her injured hand.

The ball had been struck squarely. To Nancy's satisfaction, it sailed past the trees and came to rest in the middle of the fairway some yards ahead of Miss Howard's ball. A murmur of admiration ran through the crowd.

As Nancy was leaving the tee, Sammy followed her. On a sudden inspiration she said to the lad, "Sammy, have you ever caddied for Mr. Bartescue?"

"Yes, Miss Drew. Why?"

While the girl was trying to decide how to find out from the boy whether the man had ever quizzed him about her interest in the haunted bridge, the caddy replied to her unspoken questions:

"Mr. Bartescue was always asking me about where I thought you went. I never told him about the—the scarecrow," the boy laughed.

"What did you tell him?" Nancy prodded.

"Nothing except that you seemed interested in Miss Margaret Judson who used to live near here."

At this moment the conversation was interrupted, but Nancy had learned the answer to one question which had puzzled her. A page boy from the hotel handed the girl a sealed letter.

"A message for you, Miss Drew," he announced.

Nancy accepted the envelope, but for a moment was afraid to open it. If it should prove to be a communication from Mortimer Bartescue, the man she detested, she feared her game might be ruined. She felt tempted to wait until the match was over before reading it. However, if she should do that, she probably would worry all the while about the contents. Would it not be better to learn the bad news at once?

"I may as well read it," she decided, and promptly tore open the envelope.

A broad smile played over the girl's face, for the message which she read was this:

"Good luck, Nancy. Mrs. Brownell received our message and the stage is set for her arrival."

The note was signed "Father."

CHAPTER XXV

Farewell to the Ghost

THE message puzzled Nancy for a moment; then she smiled. Her father wanted to assure her that everything was in readiness to receive Mrs. Brownell when she should visit the cabin in the woods.

The girl knew that Mr. Drew would leave no stone unturned in planning the capture of the woman who to all appearances was a member of the international jewel-thief gang.

"Good old Dad, he'll not overlook anything," she thought. "Probably by this time he's had Mrs. Brownell's telephone wires tapped and her every action will be watched. When she claims the vanity case as hers, the evidence will be complete."

Carson Drew had dispatched a telegram to New York detectives asking that they forward the stolen vanity case by airplane. Very likely he was at the airport now awaiting the package.

"Everything is moving according to our plan, so there is nothing for me to worry about except this golf match!" Nancy reflected as she studied her next shot. "I'm going to buckle down and win!"

She addressed the ball, and while the gallery watched in admiration, played a beautiful shot which her opponent could not equal. Nancy won the hole, squaring the match.

Miss Howard, grimly determined not to lose the championship, wasted no shots on the sixteenth, with the result that the hole was halved. With only two remaining to be played, the score still stood even.

As Nancy prepared to make her first shot from the seventeenth tee, Sammy sidled toward her.

"Miss Drew," he said timidly, taking a ball from his pocket, "I don't know whether or not this is the right time to tell you, but see what I found!"

"My autographed ball!" Nancy cried in delight. "Where did you find it?"

"Not far from the haunted bridge. It was hidden under some dry leaves," he replied. "Why don't you finish out the round with the autographed ball?" Sammy suggested. "It may bring you luck."

"I'd like to," Nancy declared, and turning to her opponent she requested permission to change balls.

"I have no objection," Miss Howard assured her.

Nancy was smiling as she teed up the Jimmy Harlow ball. She felt that she could not be de-

feated now. Hadn't the ball led her straight
to an absorbing mystery? Now she confidently
believed that it would bring her the silver loving cup.

So great was Nancy's elation that the pain
in her hand troubled her scarcely at all. She
became oblivious of the crowd, and heard no
comments which were made; nor was she
aware that her beautiful shots were forcing
Miss Howard to "press" and thus make serious errors. As she putted at the seventeenth
green she did not even hear Sammy murmur
excitedly:

"You're one up, Miss Drew! Take this hole
and the championship is yours!"

Nancy played "home" in true championship
style, every shot straight and true. Miss
Howard, in a desperate attempt to win, tried
too hard and sent her ball into a sandtrap.
This cost her an extra point. Nancy's ball already rested on the green scarcely three yards
from the cup.

She putted with ease and confidence. The
ball rolled so swiftly that a little gasp of
horror went up from the crowd. Many persons thought that it would end at the far side
of the green. But the ball had been struck
squarely and the aim was perfect. It dropped
with a little thump into the hole.

Miss Howard stood perfectly still for a
moment. Then she putted her own ball,
missed, and tried again. This time the ball

dropped, but already the match was lost. She reached out and grasped Nancy's hand.

"Congratulations, Miss Drew. You played a beautiful game and you deserve to win the silver cup."

The crowd cheered, and friends rushed forward to praise Nancy. At last she was led in triumph to the hotel, there to receive the handsome trophy for the women's championship.

"We knew you'd win!" Bess cried gaily. "Oh, Nancy, you were marvelous."

"Your score totaled 87," George added proudly. "It sets a new record for women here at the Deer Mountain course. And you were the youngest one in the tournament, too!"

"Will you do me a favor?" Nancy asked quickly.

George and Bess both nodded.

"We'll even clean your golf shoes for you," George chuckled. "It's an honor to perform any task for a champion."

"Never mind the kidding," Nancy rejoined, smiling. "I wish you'd take this cup and toss it in my room. I have a most important engagement."

"At the cabin?" George inquired as she relieved her chum of the trophy.

"Yes, I may be too late now, but I'd like to get there before Mrs. Brownell arrives, if I can make it."

As Nancy hastened toward the woods she

could not help but reflect that it was a pity persons of Mrs. Brownell's type chose to live by dishonest means. She caught herself wondering about the child's picture which she had seen in the jeweled vanity case. The woman had brought disgrace upon herself, but it would not be right to drag an innocent child into the affair.

Nancy approached the cabin quietly. Hearing no voices within, she opened the door. Carson Drew sprang to his feet, then laughed in relief as he saw that it was his daughter.

"I thought for a moment Mrs. Brownell had caught me napping."

"Then I am in time. She hasn't been here yet?"

"No. But she ought to be arriving soon, if at all."

"The federal agents—where are they, Dad?"

"Stationed along all the roads from her hotel. Should Mrs. Brownell decide not to come here or attempt to escape from us after being accused of the theft, she'll find every avenue cut off."

"You are convinced of her guilt, Dad?"

"Yes, her telephone wires were tapped, and we have a record which would convict her in any court. However, we wish Miss Judson to make a positive identification."

"She may never keep the appointment."

"I think her desire to obtain the vanity case

will bring her here,'' Carson Drew replied confidently.

Margaret Judson was in the adjoining room
with Mr. Haley, but at the lawyer's suggestion
she came to sit by the window while the others
secreted themselves in a closet.

Fifteen minutes elapsed, and both Nancy and
her father were growing weary of their con-
finement. Suddenly they heard Miss Judson
say in an excited undertone:

"Mrs. Brownell is coming now—and the
other woman is with her!''

"Keep perfectly calm," Carson Drew instructed crisply. "Carry out your orders to
the letter.''

The cabin door opened to admit the two
women. They glanced quickly about, and apparently satisfied that no trap had been laid
for them, addressed Miss Judson.

"I am in a great hurry," Mrs. Brownell
said. "My friend tells me that you have recovered the vanity case. Give it to me at
once."

"I have it here," Margaret Judson replied,
"but I must be certain that it actually belongs
to you."

"Let me see it.''

The case was offered for her inspection.

"Yes, it is mine.''

"You are quite certain?''

"Of course I am," Mrs. Brownell retorted
impatiently. "See, I'll show you." She

opened the lid, displaying the picture which had attracted Nancy's interest. "This is a photo of my little girl, only it has been ruined."

Carson Drew and Nancy emerged from the closet and confronted the two startled women.

"Your identification is very interesting, Mrs. Brownell," the lawyer said evenly, "for it happens that the vanity case is stolen property."

"What do you mean?" the woman gasped, backing a step away. "How could it be stolen?"

"The jeweled case was given to you by a member of a notorious smuggling gang," the lawyer said quietly, "undoubtedly as a reward for your past services in getting rid of stolen jewelry for them. But you know all this. It will suffice to say that our evidence against you is perfect."

Mrs. Brownell stared hard at Mr. Drew and knew that his words were no idle bluff. She suddenly darted toward the door, but the lawyer, prepared for just such a move, caught her firmly by the wrists. Simultaneously a federal agent appeared in the doorway, making it impossible for the Martlett woman to flee.

"You may as well tell the truth," Mr. Drew urged Mrs. Brownell as he forced her into a chair. "If you turn state's evidence your own prison term will be the lighter for it."

"It's true—the vanity case is stolen property," the accused woman admitted after a long hesitation. "I didn't mean to steal nor to have dealings with thieves, but I met a very pleasant-mannered man who induced me to do a little work for him. At first I thought it was honest work, and I accepted this jeweled vanity case in payment.

"Later on I was paid with other rich presents, until by the time I suspected the truth there was no retreating. I could only keep on with the gang. Many a time I've tried to break away, but it has been impossible."

"You will tell me the names of these persons with whom you have been dealing?"

Mrs. Brownell's eyes roved accusingly toward her companion, but Mrs. Martlett faced the group with flashing eyes.

"You can't drag me into this! I've had nothing to do with the affair. My only mistake was to be friendly with you!"

"Never mind the heroics," Carson Drew said with a smile. "Your telephone wires were tapped last night and our case against you is quite damaging, even without Mrs. Brownell's testimony."

"I will tell everything," Mrs. Brownell promised, "but only upon one condition."

"What is that?" the lawyer asked.

"My little daughter must not be dragged into this sordid mess. She is attending school in Paris and has no suspicion that her mother is anything but an honorable person. I beg of you, don't let her know what becomes of me."

"I'll do my best to keep the knowledge of your arrest from her," Mr. Drew promised soberly. "And as I said, your term should be a very light one providing you turn state's evidence."

"I will gladly make a full confession," Mrs. Brownell agreed. "Bring me paper and pen and ink."

One of the federal agents who had been trained in shorthand offered to take down the woman's words while Carson Drew questioned her. Mrs. Brownell named all the members of the international smuggling ring, and when her evidence was complete, signed the paper.

"One more question," said Mr. Drew. "Did you burn down the Judson mansion?"

"No, no, I had nothing to do with that! The fire was an accident."

"But you did enter the house with the intention of stealing the family jewels?"

"Yes, I deliberately brought up the subject with Miss Judson, inducing her to open the safe."

"Were you successful in stealing any of the pieces?"

"I took a valuable necklace, a brooch and a diamond-studded watch. The other jewels Miss Judson carried with her to her bedroom."

"What became of the stolen articles?"

"I pawned them for what they would bring."

"Have you the tickets still?" Miss Judson asked eagerly.

"Yes, I kept them, for the jewels were worth far more than I received from the pawnbroker."

Margaret Judson was overjoyed to learn that she would be able to retrieve a portion of her missing property, and after federal agents had taken away the two prisoners, she tried to thank Nancy and Mr. Drew for their kindness. Tears came to her eyes.

"In helping you we helped ourselves," the lawyer replied. "Mrs. Brownell's confession definitely closes the case."

"I think we are all rather surprised that Mortimer Bartescue had nothing to do with the jewel smuggling," Nancy commented with a smile. "There isn't a particle of evidence against him, is there, Dad?"

"No, he is just a cheap boaster."

Soon after the departure of the federal agents, Morton Wardell, Bess, George and the three boys appeared at the cabin. They had remained away only because they feared that their presence would hamper the work of the detectives. There was general rejoicing because of Miss Judson's complete vindication, and Nancy was given full credit for solving the jewel-theft case.

"One angle of the mystery still baffles me," the girl declared as they all sat grouped about old Joe Haley's bed.

"I thought everything had been explained satisfactorily," her father replied in surprise.

"I am thinking of my own special mystery, the haunted bridge," Nancy laughed. "I keep wondering who set up the scarecrow."

Mr. Haley, who had enjoyed listening to an account of the day's happenings, began to chuckle.

"I can tell you who set up the scarecrow," he announced. "I did it myself. Inquisitive boys from the golf course kept coming here and causing trouble. They bothered my animals and tramped on my flowers. I thought the scarecrow might help to keep them away."

"It certainly did," Nancy laughed. "All of the caddies decided that the bridge surely was haunted."

"The scarecrow served a useful purpose," the old man nodded. "It kept dogs away too, for they would attack the figure, barking so loudly that I'd always hear them and drive them off before they could damage my choice plants."

"When Bud and Bill repaired the bridge, they set the scarecrow back in his usual place," Ned assured the old man. "He'll serve as a guardian of your property for many years."

"There's still one thing that hasn't been explained," Bess declared. "What caused the fearful groaning noise which we heard so often?"

"I know the answer," Nancy smiled. "Wait

until we walk over the haunted bridge on our way back to the hotel and you shall have it, too.''

Margaret Judson planned to remain with Mr. Haley, caring for him until he should be able to resume his usual duties, so Ned, Bud and Bill were no longer required to remain at the cabin. They would be free to enjoy several days of fun before returning to River Heights with Nancy and her father.

As the young people prepared to leave the shack, Miss Judson drew the girls aside to tell them that she and Mr. Wardell planned to be married within a few weeks.

"We expect to rebuild the old mansion," she revealed. "Joe Haley has promised to take care of the property for us, so we hope to re-establish everything as it was before the fire."

The young people presently bade their friends farewell, and in returning to the hotel, selected their favorite route, the one which led along the ravine to the haunted bridge. Nancy drew Bess's attention to two tall trees.

"There is the explanation for the groaning sound heard so often in this vicinity."

"I don't see—" Bess began, then trailed off into silence.

The wind was rocking the treetops, and as two thick boughs rubbed together, a strange, squeaking sound was heard by those who stood below.

"When the wind is stronger, the noise takes

on the character of a groan," Nancy explained. "Sometimes the tree seems to sigh and then again almost to shriek."

Again Bess smiled in admiration of her chum's cleverness. No matter how many mysteries Nancy solved, the Marvin girl never ceased to be amazed at each new one. She was to stand aghast at the solution of the next problem, "The Clue of the Tapping Heels."

Single file the young people trooped over the bridge, feeling a trifle blue to think that their fine adventure had ended. But their spirits lifted and there was general laughter when Nancy, who came last, paused to shake the limp arm of the flapping scarecrow.

"Good-bye, old Mr. Ghost!" she addressed him gaily. "A million thanks for a very pleasant mystery!"

—The End—